I0733295

DUSKY DAHLIA

NIGHTGARDEN SAGA #5

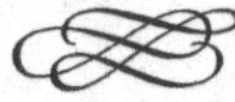

LUCY HOLDEN

FEHU PRESS

Copyright © 2021 by Paula Constant writing as Lucy Holden

All rights reserved.

No part of this book may be reproduced in any form or by any electronic or mechanical means, including information storage and retrieval systems, without written permission from the author, except for the use of brief quotations in a book review.

For all those we have lost
You are remembered, and you are loved
Always

PREVIOUS TITLES

The Nightgarden Saga books in order:

Red Magnolia
Moon Vine
Poison Berry
Bayou Rose
Dusky Dahlia
Blue Lilies
Night Shade

PROLOGUE

ear Tessa,

THE MOON IS HIGH OVER THE WATER, AND THE WORLD IS ASLEEP. Antoine is gone, hunting as he often does in the early hours when he knows it won't disturb me. I'm glad he isn't here. I woke from a dream so startling it still feels real, and I'm writing to you because you are the only person I can trust with it.

Lately, it seems I hear you on the wind, in the water, more than ever before. Sometimes when my hands are in the earth or the breeze moves, I hear your laugh, so soft it is there and gone by the time I've turned to find you. I see your face in the billowing cloud over the river in the late afternoon. The birds chatter in your voice, and there are days I'm so certain you are beside me that I begin to speak before I realize it's only my imagination.

I thought the longing for you would grow less with years, not greater. I feel old, Tessa, like I've lived a hundred lifetimes instead of barely a quarter of one. When I see our friends preparing for college, their world feels a universe removed from mine. There are no surprises in their choices. Jeremiah and Avery are both going to Ole Miss in Oxford, Jeremiah studying history, Avery pre-med. Cass, sadly, isn't going to college at all. I know she was planning to study music. After everything that has happened, though, she doesn't really trust herself near humans. And I don't think she likes being away from Connor. They're living in her mom's old house. If Avery has spent the summer being brittle and distant with me, Cass is simply sad. Connor told me not to ask about it, so I haven't.

Callie has spent much of the summer with Jeremiah. I think she will miss him a lot when he goes.

They all seem so distant from me and the odd life I lead. Yours has become the most real voice in my world, Tessa, as strange as that might sound. Which is why you're the only person in whom I can confide the truth about my dream last night.

In my dream it was also late at night. I was sitting on a rock by a vast, still sea. Moonlight rippled across the surface. All about me was silent emptiness, just the moon and me amid the indigo night, the water still as glass. Gradually I became aware of something drawing me forward, across the water, to where the moonbeam reflection was most brilliant. I traveled across the water as if carried on the moonbeam itself, an intense rush of energy pulling me to where it shone the brightest. The light grew stronger, until a brilliant blaze drenched every cell of my body, overwhelming my every sense until the light was all there was. Below me the still water began to churn. For the longest time, I was held in that euphoric blaze of light, suspended over a wild sea, surrounded and filled by a force stronger than any I've ever felt. Then, as suddenly as it had come, the light was gone, the moon returned to a pale disk in the sky, the sea quiet. I found myself back on the rock, staring out at the still, glassy surface, as undisturbed as it had been before I was drawn to its center.

I woke a moment after that.

I'm writing it down before I forget, though I suspect I will remember every moment of that dream for the rest of my life.

It's been six weeks since the night Antoine drank from me. I knew there was something special about that night. Something unlike the other times we'd been together, something beyond us both, that seemed to draw us to one another with the inevitability of magnets, made us lose ourselves in a melding of soul and body unlike any force I've either known or imagined.

When I woke after my dream last night, I knew what that something was.

I'm pregnant, Tessa.

No matter how impossible or improbable, that's the truth. It's what I felt in the dream and know in my body.

I'm pregnant. Even saying it sounds insane.

And if it sounds that way to me—how on earth am I going to tell anyone else?

Your twin,
Harper

CHAPTER 1

SECRETS

There's nothing simple about buying a pregnancy test in a small town.

The main drugstore in Deepwater Hollow is owned by Avery's parents. I've barely seen Avery for weeks, and I suspect Mr. and Mrs. Fairweather aren't my greatest fans. They already blame me for Avery's relationship with Remy. Avery's parents worked hard to send themselves to college, then returned to make something of themselves in a town that always looked down on them. They have high aspirations for Avery that definitely don't include a tattooed man from the bayou with a dubious past. Somehow I doubt buying a pregnancy test is likely to improve my standing with them.

I go to the drugstore on a day when I know they usually work out back and have an assistant on the desk. When the bell on the door jangles to announce my presence, however, it is Avery I find behind the counter. My heart sinks. I can't exactly turn around and leave again, so I plaster a smile on my face and grab some random hand cream from the shelf on my way to the counter. I haven't seen Avery for weeks. I'm struck by how sad she looks, her usually glossy hair dull and in a messy braid, her face pale.

"Hey," I say tentatively.

"Hey." She gives me a small smile as she rings up the hand cream. I try not to look at the row of pregnancy test boxes on the shelf nearby. "I'm sorry I haven't called." She stares down at the counter, fiddling with the cream, something clearly on her mind.

"Avery?" She looks up, and the realization that she is fighting back tears pushes my own dilemma momentarily to the back of my mind. "What's wrong?"

She glances over her shoulder to where her parents are watching us beadily through the glass window. "Remy and I broke up." The watchful faces of her parents and the way she whispers it gives me a fair idea of what might be the cause of the breakup.

"Was it because of your parents?"

Avery shrugs. "Them. And other things." She glances up as if she wants to say more, but then shakes her head and dashes away a stray tear. "Anyhow, I'm off to the University of Mississippi·soon. And everyone knows long-distance relationships don't work." Her smile is barely a ghost.

I don't blame her for not wanting to talk about it. I know better than anyone the world of secrets we share. It's not for me to judge those kept by others. I cover her hand briefly with my own.

"I'm so sorry, Avery." I mean it. I know she loves Remy, and I'm pretty sure he never got over his luck in landing someone as gorgeous and smart as Avery. I'm sad for them both. "At least you'll have a friend at college. Jeremiah is going to Ole Miss as well."

"He is?" Avery's face lights up. "What's he studying?"

"History." I smile wryly. "Turns out Tate coming to Deepwater High was the best thing that could have happened to Jeremiah. He's spent most of the summer glued to Tate's side, reading books I can't even lift, they're so heavy. He's currently obsessed with the French Revolution, and he's super excited because Ramon, an old friend of Tate's who saw the whole Napoleonic era live and in technicolor, is coming to visit." When Avery looks confused, I hold up my hands. "Don't ask me. History wasn't my subject either. But I guess one bonus with immortal friends is having prime source material on hand. Jeremiah and Callie are ridiculously excited about meeting Ramon. It helps that Callie speaks French and Spanish. She taught herself, apparently." I shake my head. I sometimes suspect Callie is hiding an entirely different person under her gangster image. The first day she began speaking to Antoine in passable French, we both stared at her in open-mouthed astonishment, but Callie just shrugged and said she'd picked it up from a Cajun boyfriend her mother had when she was a kid. Spanish she'd learned from the Mexican kids at her boxing club. "I like the way languages work," she told us, leaving Antoine and I speechless. I realize that Avery, however, doesn't seem quite so impressed.

"So that skinny kid is still hanging around Jeremiah," she sniffs.

"Callie has been a good friend to Jeremiah." Whereas Avery, I can't help but think, has been all too willing to exploit Jeremiah's almost slavish devotion when it suits her, only to discard him without a thought when something better comes along. Avery, though, true to form, is oblivious to my subtle rebuke.

"I'll call Jeremiah when I get off work." She's already looking more like her old self. "It will be good to have at least one friend at college." She glances at the hand cream. "Have you been gardening too much again?"

"Occupational hazard," I lie, forcing a smile. "Connor and I are getting a greenhouse set up so I can start a nursery."

"So you're really going to just stay here, in Deepwater? With

—him?" She doesn't need to say Antoine's name. I can see the mixed emotions on her face, feel the envy, guilt, and curiosity wash through her. It's one of the many things I've become accustomed to over the summer, this immediate understanding of what others are feeling. It's not always comfortable. Sometimes I react to what I know people feel, rather than what they say. It's made for some uncomfortable interactions at times. It took me a while to understand that people don't always want to be understood. So I choose my words carefully now.

"I've never wanted to go to college, Avery. You know that. All I've ever wanted to do is paint and grow things. I'm happy doing that right where I am. And yes, for now at least, Antoine and I are together." I pick up my hand cream. "But I guess we all know things change."

"Sure." She gives me a forced smile. "Well, I'll come see y'all before I go." She pauses. "Have you seen much of Cass?"

"Not a whole lot." I'm careful with what I say. "She's had to make a lot of adjustments, I guess."

"Haven't we all," Avery mutters, unable to keep a note of resentment from her tone. I'm guessing she still holds Cass responsible for Connor turning into a wolf and causing problems for Remy in leading the bayou pack. It's a drama I can't do anything about, and anyhow, I've more pressing matters on my mind—like where else I can buy a pregnancy test in a town where everyone seems to notice everything.

I'm saved from an awkward exit by someone else needing to be served, and I slip from the drugstore with a little wave. There's another, smaller drugstore on Second St. I'd avoided it because it's close to Witch Way, the shop once run by Cass's mom. I thought Cass would close it after her mom's terrible death at Keziah's hands, but she hasn't. I think it's given her something to do while she's working out what her life is going to be. Given that it will be an immortal life, I guess it's no small question.

Sure enough, just as I'm getting out of my Mustang in front of the drugstore, Cass comes out of Witch Way. I force a smile.

"I've just seen Avery," I say by way of greeting. "She and Remy have split up, it seems."

"Oh, no!" Cass looks genuinely sympathetic, though I know for a fact Avery has barely returned her calls this summer. Cass is just kind, even now, after living with Keziah's blood in her veins and months of her mind control. "Do you know why?"

"She mentioned college and long distance." I realize my mistake instantly. Cass turns away abruptly, but not before I see how her face closes over and feel the wave of frustration and loneliness inside her. "I'm sorry, Cass," I say quietly. "That was insensitive."

"It isn't your fault." Cass gives me a false, bright smile that I know better than to question. "As Connor says, in time I'll be able to study whatever I want. Just not quite yet." I nod, figuring silence is the only diplomatic response to that. For all her kindness, Cass is still a vampire and a savage one at that. I know she struggles with urges that Antoine says can take years, if not decades, to settle. At least in the shop she can walk away or close the door. A lecture hall, I guess, isn't quite so simple.

"Anyway. Did you come just to say hi?"

"Yes," I lie, with a bright smile of my own. "Just checking in."

"I'm fine, Harper. Really. You don't all need to check on me every second." Cass's eyes flash, and I get a momentary glimpse of the killer within. I nod again and step back.

"Sure," I say gently. "I'll see you round, Cass." She doesn't answer, but I suspect that's more because she doesn't want me to see her cry than because she's actually mad at me. I get back into the Mustang silently and give the drugstore a rueful glance.

In the end, I drive an hour to the next town to buy the test.

At a roadside gas station, I go into the bathroom and stare at the little white stick. I'd always thought it would take a long time for the results to appear.

It doesn't.

In a matter of seconds, I'm staring at two, unmistakably bright pink lines.

The test tells me what I already know—and what I equally know to be impossible.

I'm pregnant.

I drive home slowly, wonder and terror churning inside me.

CHAPTER 2

SEEDLINGS

$\mathcal{A}$ntoine calls as I pull into the driveway. "I'm going to be late. The engine on the boat failed. It's going to take a while to fix." I can hear Jeremiah laughing in the background.

"You're on the river," I say, smiling.

"We'll be on the river a while yet," Jeremiah calls.

"He seems to be enjoying this."

"Oh, he is." Antoine's tone is light. "He's taking great delight in reminding me that engines don't care whether I'm immortal or not." I can picture Antoine as he speaks, eyes caught in the last rays of the sun, hair tousled by the river air. I feel a sudden, visceral tug of longing.

"Come home soon."

His tone drops a notch, sending a tremor down my spine. "I will."

"Oh, stop it," says Jeremiah impatiently in the background. "She'll still be there when you get home." I hang up to the sound of their banter, smiling to myself. Over a long summer in which nothing was more constant than uncertainty, Jeremiah's obvious delight in Tate and Antoine's company has been a source of joy. He's spent his days working with Connor on the mansion and his evenings pouring over history books with Tate, Antoine, and Callie. I've never seen someone so enamored of his college reading list. I'd never realized how much he loved history, but I suspect he hadn't either, until the arrival of both Tate and Callie, who between them seem to have brought his passion to the surface.

"You seem deep in thought." I spin around to find Connor behind me. The day is fading, and my brother has appeared as silently as the dusk shadows. I smile without looking directly at him and nod instead at the steel structure on the empty land beside the mansion. "The greenhouse is coming along."

"It's going to be all you asked for, I hope." Connor looks at it in satisfaction. "And you've already made a good start on the seedlings." He nods at the neat rows of pots by the night garden. He casts me a sideways glance. "But I get the feeling it isn't plants you're thinking about."

"Would you do me a favor?" I hand him my phone. "Would you take a photo of me, right now, here in the garden?"

"Sure." Connor looks at me quizzically as I pose. "Any particular reason?"

"I just want to remember this moment." I smile into the camera. "When everything is still at the beginning." My hand sneaks unconsciously down to my belly. I pull it away before Connor can notice.

"I'd say it's a lot further along than the beginning," Connor says. My heart almost stops, but when I look up he is smiling, and I realize he was talking about the garden rather than my belly. I take a shaky breath and keep smiling as he takes a few photos of me there. When he's done, I look at the smiling figure on the screen, marveling that it isn't completely obvious to everyone that I am different, that I carry a life within me now.

"I saw Cass today," I say, not least to distract myself from my thoughts. "She's not doing so well, with everyone heading off to college."

Connor's smile fades. "No," he says shortly. "She isn't." His smile is as forced as Cass's was earlier today. "Well." He turns back toward the mansion. "I'll leave you to it." I watch him walk away, the long, graceful lope that has become his natural gait since he transformed into a wolf. My brother is still my brother, but I never forget that, like all of us it seems, he is also so much more now. I know his inability to help Cass is frustrating and worrying for him. But he doesn't share that part of his life with me anymore. He and Cass are a unit now, as tightly bound as Antoine and I are. There are things only they share. I understand it and respect their privacy, but Connor is my brother, and it hurts to see him so obviously in pain, just as it does to see Cass's misery.

In the silence following his departure, I try to think of how I am going to tell Antoine that I'm pregnant.

He will say it's impossible.

I already know this. I've thought of almost nothing else since I woke from that dream. I can almost hear his arguments. Perhaps that's why I asked Connor to take the photo of me in the garden. I want a record of this moment, the brief pause when I can be alone with the miracle inside me before chaos erupts, which it surely will when I break the news.

My hand steals down to cover my belly again. I know I'm being fanciful, but it genuinely seems as if I can feel the life within me, just as I can when I plant a seed deep in the earth. It's a certain warmth, an inner density, the sensation of energy and matter gathering within. That blazing light that flooded my body. *That was you, little one,* I think, holding my belly in wonder. *That was you coming to me, from wherever it is souls arrive. From God, I guess.* I recognize the irony of thinking of God when I'm talking about a baby conceived by a vampire and Abatey incarnate. *An immortal killer and the modern embodiment of an ancient deity.* I shake my head. *What manner of miracle does such a union create?*

That thought should scare me, I know. But it doesn't, or at least, not for long. Some other inner certainty settles over me every time I touch my belly or think of the little pink lines on the test. It's too wondrous a miracle for me to feel afraid. I guess I can only hope Antoine feels the same.

I will tell him tonight, I decide. When he gets home. It's only been one day, but I feel as if I've been hugging the knowledge to myself for an eternity. I've had my private moment to come to terms with it. Now I want to share it with Antoine, no matter how shocked I know he will be.

The soft fragrance of red magnolia touches my face. "I wish you were here, Tessa," I whisper, an ache catching in my throat. "I wish I could share this miracle with you. I wish my little one could know you."

I'm here.

Her voice is so real I swing around, startled, then half smile at my own fancy. "It seems so real sometimes." I touch the petals of the magnolia. "Here, in the garden. As if you were in the soil, on the breeze. You told me that, Tessa." My eyes fill with tears as I remember that last day in the hospital, before Tessa ceased speaking. "You said I'd always find you on the breeze, in the flowers. You told me to put some of your ashes in my garden, so you'd always be with me. I couldn't even hear you at the time." I'm crying now, scalding hot tears I can't seem to control. "But I did what you asked, Tessa. I put you in the earth here. And I do feel you. Every day, with every breeze. Sometimes I feel you so strongly I would swear your hand is on mine, that you're standing right by me. I miss you so damned much, Tessa."

Night has fallen, and I draw a shuddering breath. I'm shaken by the sudden rush of emotion. I look around self-consciously, relieved nobody witnessed my little meltdown. *I guess it's hormones.* Don't they say that pregnant women are completely overly emotional? Just the thought feels overwhelming. I'm struggling not to cry again.

I'm going to need to get a grip.

I realize with a grimace that Connor's truck is still parked outside the mansion; I don't really feel up to his scrutiny. Then I realize Tate's vehicle is there as well and, as I take that in, Antoine's boat glides to a halt at the jetty below, and he leaps from it as Jeremiah tosses him the rope.

Great, I think resignedly. *Just what I need—a roomful of people with supernatural senses of observation.*

But for once, Antoine's attention isn't entirely focused on me as he strides to my side and kisses me in an unusually perfunctory manner. "Is Tate here yet?"

"I think so." I look up at his face, see the slate-gray eyes soften as his arms tighten around me briefly. "I thought you were going to be late," I say, my arms around his neck. He pulls me closer briefly and kisses me again, in a way that makes my breath hitch.

"I was. But then Tate called. It seems we have a visitor, so I had to deprive Jeremiah of the joy of watching me pretend to struggle with the engine." Despite his levity, there is a shadow behind his eyes.

"Ramon is here already?" Last I knew, Tate's friend was due to arrive in a week or so.

"Not Ramon." We walk toward the mansion, Antoine's arm still holding me close to his side. "Someone else."

I guess my secret is going to need to wait a while longer.

CHAPTER 3

IARA

The kitchen is Connor's current work in progress, so we gather instead in the recently renovated state room that has become our new living area. The French windows open onto the back porch, where I've set up a makeshift kitchen while Connor renovates the other one. The state room has high ceilings, marble tiles, and a carved chaise longue that Connor rescued from an antique store. On the chaise rests one of the most startlingly beautiful young women I've ever seen. She has sloping almond eyes, high cheekbones, olive skin that suggests Latin heritage, and a figure lush and curvaceous enough to make Jeremiah's eyes widen then move away hastily, as if even looking at such a body makes him self-conscious. She's wearing an ancient, faded T-shirt over somewhat unflattering shorts, teamed with dirty rubber flip-flops. Tate stands beside her, his hand resting lightly on her shoulder.

"This is Iara," he says as we enter.

It takes little more than one glance for me to realize that Iara is a vampire. By now, I'm highly attuned to their uncanny beauty. More than that, my newly awakened senses have discovered that vampires hum at a slightly different frequency than humans. There is something finer, higher, in their energy field that is both less dense and yet more durable than that of humans. I'm still learning to read such things, but I feel them instantly. I sense something else in Iara's field—that she is new to this immortal life.

"The wolves found Iara in the bayou, lost and confused," Tate says before we have a chance to ask. "Remy called me instead of killing her," he answers Antoine's unspoken question, "because she told him she was looking for me."

"Why?" Antoine turns to the newcomer, who bursts into a voluble torrent of Spanish that both Antoine and Tate seem to follow without difficulty. The rest of us just watch in silence, until Callie, who has an unsettling ability to disappear into the background until she decides to be noticed, begins to translate.

"She came here with Ramon," Callie says in a low voice. "He took her from her village in Venezuela very recently, no more than a few weeks ago. They were traveling here to meet him." Callie nods at Tate, not taking her eyes from Iara. "But earlier tonight, as they were about to cross the river from Louisiana to Mississippi, a woman came—another of their kind. Vampire," Callie adds, somewhat unnecessarily. "The woman was very strong. She overcame Ramon. Killed him. Then the wolves came."

"Keziah," I say flatly. Antoine nods. He strides from the room and comes back a moment later, holding up the sketch I once drew of Keziah's face, back when she had still been bound in our cellar and appearing to me only in dreams. It seems like a lifetime ago, before any of this world was real to me.

"Is this the face you saw?" Antoine asks Iara in Spanish. She nods, her eyes wide.

Tate passes a hand over his face. "I didn't think to tell Ramon that Keziah was here. I thought he'd call before he arrived. And I didn't expect Keziah to have an interest in him, anyway." He shakes his head. "Ramon was ancient," he says quietly. "And one of my oldest friends. He was a good man."

"I'm sorry." Antoine's hand rests briefly on Tate's shoulder.

"We have to take care of her," Tate says, meeting Antoine's eyes over Iara's head. "We can't just let her loose here. She's from a Venezuelan backwater; she'll be completely lost in our world. Ramon wouldn't have made her without reason." He frowns for a moment. "I'm surprised he made her at all, frankly. He always said he'd never make another of our kind." His eyes rest briefly on Iara, as if searching for answers. Iara meets his gaze with a wide-eyed naivety that is oddly touching. Tate smiles at her reassuringly before turning back to Antoine.

"Regardless, we can't abandon her, Antoine. Iara's lost her Maker and is in a foreign country. I can't just tell her to go."

"Just what we need," mutters Connor. "Another vampire."

He folds his arms and meets Tate's reproving glance with a belligerent look of his own. "What?" he says, unrepentant. "You think we don't already have enough supernatural around here?"

"Connor." It's Callie who speaks. "She's scared," she says quietly, looking at our brother. "And she's alone."

Connor clicks his tongue and looks away, but he doesn't argue. We all know how that feels. It was only recently that Connor rejected Callie when she needed help. He's learned from that. Connor won't turn Iara away, even if he might want to.

My hand steals to my belly again. I catch it just in time and look around quickly, relieved when no one seems to have noticed. It's Callie saying the words *scared* and *alone*, I realize, that made me think again of my little miracle. Suddenly, I just can't hold on to that secret anymore. I don't want to be alone with it. I want Antoine to know, to be aware.

"It's getting late," I announce. Everyone looks at me in

surprise. It's barely eight. I color faintly. "Let's sleep on it. Iara can stay with us tonight, and we can talk in the morning."

"No," Tate says, somewhat abruptly. As if realizing how he sounds, he adds in a slightly gentler tone, "Ramon was my friend. Iara can stay with me." He turns to Callie. "Will you come? It may help for her to have a woman who speaks her language." When she nods, Tate extends his hands to Iara and lifts her gently to her feet, smiling reassuringly. Her eyes glow, and she moves instinctively to his side, undoubtedly feeling the same warm acceptance we all do in Tate's presence, the gift of the inherent diplomat he is. A moment later they are gone, taking Callie and Jeremiah with them. Tate has been living at the river house too. Connor nods at Antoine and me as he leaves as silently as he came.

"So." I turn to find Antoine watching me quizzically, his arms folded as he leans against the doorframe. "Are you going to tell me why you evicted everyone so abruptly, or am I supposed to guess?"

I give a choked laugh. "I doubt you'd ever guess. Not even in four lifetimes."

His dark eyes glow with curiosity. "Perhaps you'd better tell me, then." He reaches out and brushes his thumb across my cheekbone in a gesture that makes my heart twist. I take a deep breath, feeling a strange flutter of excitement and uncertainty in my solar plexus.

"I know you won't believe me," I start.

"Try me." He folds his arms again, watching me intently.

"It will seem impossible—"

"Just tell me, Harper."

"—but I've thought it through, and I think I know how it happened—"

"Harper." His eye glitter dangerously. "Speak."

I take another breath. "I'm pregnant."

For a moment there is only an odd, charged silence, the air

crackling with the words. Antoine is so still he seems carved from stone, shock chasing all pretense of humanity from his features. His eyes bore into mine, gold and slate shifting in their depths, not really seeing me.

Finally he speaks. "That's impossible," he says flatly.

With an effort, I manage not to roll my eyes.

"You can't be—" He stops, unable to bring himself to say the word, and his eyes drift down to where my hand covers my belly. "You can't be," he says again, more uncertainly this time.

"I am." I watch him warily. "I took a test. More than one, actually." In fact, I took four, even though I already knew what they'd say. I had to be sure.

Taking advantage of his silence, I press on. "I know how it happened. It was just after your blood had activated mine, when you drank from me. Do you remember what you said? That my blood felt unlike anything you'd ever known. That it was like being human—only more so, as if every cell of your body was alive. I remember being drawn toward you that whole day, almost as if it was beyond my control. And when we were together that night, you said it was like—"

"Magic," he breathes, staring at me. "It was like magic." I nod slowly. We stare at each other for a long moment, and I see the pieces joining up in his mind, the slow awareness dawning in his eyes. "And you think that is what happened," he says. "That because of your blood—for one night, at least—I really *was* human, my body functioning as a normal man's would?"

"Hardly normal," I say, unable to hide a small smile, but he doesn't seem to notice the joke.

"That night," he says, talking to himself as much as to me, "and the next day, it was like we were in another world, you and I."

"I didn't know where you left off and I began." I reach out and grasp his hand. "I knew it was extraordinary. Everything about that night, the way we were drawn to one another. You said it was like the power of the earth itself inside you, and I could feel it, surging between us."

"I've never felt anything like it," he says roughly, "not ever." His eyes travel down to my belly again. "You're sure," he says, and for the first time, I hear the wonder in his voice.

"I'm sure." Gently I take his hand and place it on my belly, and he stares down at it, fascination making his eyes cobalt. "It's a miracle," I say softly. "It's our miracle, Antoine."

His eyes travel back up to my face. "I don't know whether to be ecstatic or terrified," he says, in such an uncertain voice I laugh aloud.

"Be ecstatic," I murmur, reaching up to touch his lips with my own. "Be overjoyed. Be amazed. It truly is a miracle, Antoine." Oddly, I feel more certain than I ever have, of anything. "I dreamed it, even before I took the test that confirmed it."

"You dreamed it?" He pulls back, examining my face.

"Come to the garden, and I'll tell you all about it."

I lead him out into the night, and in the end, we talk for hours. I don't just tell him about the dream. I tell him how I felt the night he took me in the night garden, how I had a sense of inevitability the whole time, as if being with him that night was a tide I couldn't hold back. I tell him how it felt in the dream, to have the blazing light fill my body, and that I'd known, when I woke, that I was pregnant. We talk all night, walking back and forth from the river to the mansion, excited and charged, sleep so far away as to be impossible. Finally, as dawn approaches, we're lying in the warm grass beneath the red magnolia that grows near the jetty, Antoine's head resting gently on my belly, as if he's afraid to let the weight of it fall fully on my body. My hand is curled in his.

"Harper." His voice is hesitant. "What if—" he breaks off abruptly, as if regretting that he started, but I know what he means.

"What if we've created something supernatural?" His head shifts on my body as he nods. "I think that is inevitable," I say quietly. "How could it be otherwise, with a vampire father and a nature spirit mother?"

"But what if this baby isn't just—supernatural?"

"I know what you're afraid of." I stroke his face, staring up into the infinite blue of the predawn. "Of course I've wondered about the dangers, a baby with powers we don't understand and can't control. But Antoine—you didn't feel the light I did, in the dream. There was nothing dark in that presence. It was the most glorious, exhilarating, wondrous thing I've ever felt. Our baby won't be something dark, Antoine. She's a miracle. I can feel it."

"She?"

I nod, a slow smile curving my mouth. "I feel that, too. It's a girl. I'm certain of it."

"A baby girl." Antoine's hand roams over my belly, his tone full of wonder. "I can barely imagine it." His hand stills and he props himself up, eyes dark with concern. "But this is unfair. You're so young, Harper. You can't have imagined this being your life."

"Stop." I cup his face with my hand. "Don't you understand?" I say softly. "I've lost my entire family, Antoine. My mom, my sister. Even Connor isn't really my brother anymore, not like he once was. And now I have a chance to have that again. To have a family of my own. To live with you, make a life with you. How can you imagine that this is anything other than the greatest blessing life could give me? I don't just want this baby, Antoine. I want her—and you—more than I've ever wanted anything in my life."

We grip hands as dawn threads the horizon, staring at one another, eyes alight with a future neither of us could ever have imagined.

"One thing is certain," says Antoine, glancing down at the

emerald on my finger and smiling wryly. "I will have to marry you again. In public, this time. I won't have anyone saying our baby isn't a Marigny." In the gray light of dawn, the air around us moves and we both leap to our feet, startled, to find Connor staring at us, his face gaunt.

"Baby?" he says harshly. "What baby?"

CHAPTER 4

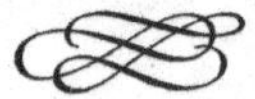

MIRACLES

"You're early," I stammer. My face is flaming. Even Antoine looks uncharacteristically awkward.

"It's summer, Harper. I've been here before dawn every day." He looks grimly between Antoine and me. "What baby?" he asks again.

"We weren't going to say anything yet," I begin.

"We?" Connor repeats flatly. His eyes swivel to Antoine. "Harper is pregnant with your baby? You're telling me that is somehow possible?"

"We don't really understand it either," says Antoine quietly.

"It's to do with my blood." My words tumble out awkwardly. "Something in it changed after I drank from Antoine. Then, when Antoine drank from me again, it changed him, too. For a while, at least." My voice trails off. "I don't know how to explain it."

"A baby," Connor says slowly. "You're going to have a baby." For a moment his mouth twists into a strange, pained smile. "That's amazing." His voice is slightly choked. A gleam of something I can't quite read flashes in his eyes. "Weird and impossible—but incredible, too." The tight, nervous knot inside my chest releases slightly, and I breathe for the first time since my brother found us. The relief is short-lived. Connor glances over his shoulder, and the light in his face is chased away like a river cloud on a morning breeze. "Please don't tell Cass." His voice is low and urgent. "Not yet, at least. I need time to prepare her."

But he's too late. We've been talking with our faces turned up the slope, toward the mansion. Cass is standing behind us, among the riverside trees, holding a brown paper bag in one hand.

"To prepare me for what?"

I close my eyes briefly, wincing inwardly. "You forgot your lunch," Cass says to Connor, but her eyes are fixed on me. "What is it that you don't want to tell me?"

"Cass—" My brother puts out a placating hand, but Cass sidesteps his reach.

"Don't, Connor," she says quietly. "You can't protect me from everything." She looks at me again. "What is it?"

I glance at Antoine. This definitely isn't the way I imagined breaking this news. I've barely begun to understand it myself. I don't feel ready for the scrutiny of others, not yet. Antoine lifts his eyebrows in question, and I nod slightly, moving closer to him, feeling the comforting weight of his hand on my lower back.

"As strange as it sounds," Antoine says quietly, "it seems that Harper is pregnant, Cass."

Cass's face is still as marble, her eyes flat and dark. "Pregnant," she repeats flatly. Nothing moves in her expression. I have no idea what she is thinking. For a moment, there is only the hesitant chirruping of morning birds and the soft rustle of leaves on the river breeze. Then Cass looks at Antoine. "Her blood," she breathes. She looks back at me, and now there is a light in her eyes. "It's because he drank your blood, isn't it, Harper?" I nod, pleased she seems to be taking it so well. I'm aware of Antoine shifting uneasily beside me, but I don't realize why until Cass speaks again. "Then it's possible," she breathes, and now her eyes are gleaming with excitement. "Your blood can actually make us human?"

"Cass—" Connor puts out a hand, but Cass shakes him off. I can see the pain in Connor's eyes, and I realize with horrible clarity that this is what he was trying to protect Cass from, the terrible weight of this hope, that my brother already knows, instinctively, is doomed to fail.

"It worked for you." Cass is talking to Antoine now. "If it worked once, then it can work again."

"I'm a man, Cass." Antoine's voice is gentle, but nonetheless direct. "I felt Harper's blood work within me for a matter of hours, the traces there for perhaps a couple of days. You know it yourself—you've felt it. For me, that was long enough. But for you, for a woman—Cass, you'd need to have that blood inside you every moment of every day, for nine months." He doesn't look away from the hope in her eyes. "It couldn't work, Cass. Harper would never survive that. She couldn't survive that. Not in the quantities you would need. The moment it stopped working—" his voice breaks off, leaving a terrible silence. In it lies the horrifying images of what happens to a human baby trapped inside a dead body that is unable to sustain it, to change and evolve and bring it sustenance. I shudder, my hand going involuntarily to my belly. As Cass's eyes follow the gesture, I realize my mistake.

"Cass—" I start, reaching for her, but I'm too late. Cass gives a choked sob and backs away, staring at my belly. Before any of us can speak, she turns and disappears into the trees. Cursing under his breath, my brother leaps into the air, sending his clothes flying as he transforms mid-leap. A moment later the black wolf has disappeared after Cass, leaving Antoine and me staring in their wake.

"That went well," he murmurs dryly.

"Poor Cass." I put my head in my hands. "Maybe it could

work, Antoine. If we planned it carefully, worked out exactly how much blood she would need—"

"No," says Antoine, so sharply I look up at him. His face has gone uncharacteristically pale. "No, Harper," he says, shaking his head. He takes my hand and leads me toward the mansion. "We're going to have a baby that is nothing short of a miracle." I can hear the tension in his voice. "Neither of us knows how this pregnancy will affect you, if you will suffer, or if the baby—" he breaks off, rubbing a hand over his face, as unwilling as I am to even contemplate what terrible options we may face in the coming months. "We don't know," he finishes lamely. "Even if what Cass was thinking is possible, which I don't believe any of us realistically think it is, now is not the time to so much as contemplate it. Promise me, Harper." We have been walking as he talked, and now I face him on the back porch. He takes my hands. "All that matters to me, Harper, is you and our baby. Keeping you both safe. We both know we already face threats enough, without creating more danger. I don't even want to think about what Keziah will do if she finds out about this."

I shudder for the second time that morning. "I've been trying not to think of Keziah," I admit.

"At first I thought we should keep this a secret," Antoine says, frowning. "At least until we know more about it. But now that Cass knows . . . perhaps we should tell Tate and Jeremiah. I can't be with you all the time, Harper. We'll need all the help we can get if we are going to keep you safe."

"I don't know that I'm ready to tell people." I touch my belly, trying to imagine what is happening inside me, feeling the quiet wonder I've yet to become used to. "Can't we keep this to ourselves for just a little longer?"

I've barely finished speaking when the sound of an engine rumbles in the distance. "That's Jeremiah's motorcycle." Antoine's face twists into a wry smile. "And he has Callie aboard. I think it's a little late to keep it to ourselves."

CHAPTER 5

SPIRITS

Jeremiah and Callie take the news better than I expect. In fact, apart from their wide eyes, they barely react at all.

"I wonder if there are legends about this." Callie looks at Jeremiah. "I'll start searching, see what I can find." She pulls out her laptop.

Jeremiah frowns. "It's a pity I'm off to college in a few days. You guys are going to need all the help you can get." He pulls out his phone. "Have you told Tate yet? He might have some ideas."

"I've asked him to come," says Antoine.

"What about Avery?"

"I've texted her. She should be here soon. You two seem to be taking this awfully well," I say, looking between them. Callie shrugs.

"We've gotten good with weird," she says, without looking up from her laptop research.

Tate and Iara arrive together. Iara looks a little less woebegone than yesterday, helped by a clean T-shirt and skirt that I suspect Tate picked out for her. He seems very protective of her. I imagine he is still mourning his friend. Antoine told me that

28

Tate had known Ramon for over two centuries. They even lived together for a time, as a family. It's no wonder he sees Iara as his responsibility.

Antoine breaks the news to Tate outside, away from Iara, murmuring a warning to Jeremiah and Callie as well. "Let's not share it with her for now," he says to me as he leads Tate outside. "Not until we know more about her, at least."

I go upstairs to shower and change before Avery arrives, and also because after the long, sleep-deprived night, I'm wired and jittery and need to take a beat, try to let my head catch up with all that is happening. None of it feels quite real. It's almost as if the real thing is the dream I had, of being in the middle of a darkened sea as light filled my body. The actuality of being pregnant, of telling others and dealing with the future, feels like the dream. I want to dive into the indigo peace where there is only myself and the life within me, floating together on a midnight sea.

Instead I dress slowly, descending the stairs to the sound of Avery's voice on the back porch. As I get closer, I hear another voice. Iara is talking in rapid Spanish to Callie.

"What is it?" I look between them. Tate and Antoine are still some distance away, their heads together, and by the rigid tension in their bodies, I suspect their conversation isn't going well. Iara is staring at Avery in fascination.

"Apparently she can see a spirit around me," Avery says, rolling her eyes. "As if we didn't already know that."

"Not just one spirit," Callie corrects, still listening closely to Iara. "Lots of them. She says they're all around you."

"So what?" Avery shrugs. "It's not like they're doing any good, if I can't actually understand them. Believe me, I've tried." She turns her back on Iara, whose face falls. I wince. Avery can be incredibly insensitive at times, even if I suspect her dismissal is born more from hurt than any real intention to wound Iara. I know Avery has been working with Lori, Remy's mother, to try to better understand her powers—but also that she's had limited success. Avery isn't accustomed to being less than perfect at anything. It can't be easy, particularly when she's surrounded by supernatural creatures.

"What did you want to talk to me about so early, anyhow? I've still got to pack for college."

I lead her away from Iara's scrutiny and the tense figures of Antoine and Tate, out the front and away from supernatural ears, beneath the canopy of live oak. I take a deep breath. "I know this will sound crazy," I start.

Minutes later, Avery is gaping at me in utter shock; then her mouth closes, and her eyes grow hard. I sigh inwardly. I knew this wouldn't be easy, but did it have to be quite so difficult, every time? Even though I'm braced for hostility, Avery's response still takes me by surprise.

"Do you know why Remy and I broke up?"

"You told me it was because of the distance. And your parents."

"Those were just excuses." Avery's eyes glitter dangerously. "Because I didn't want to tell anyone that Remy ditched me."

"Breaking up was Remy's idea?" I can't hide my surprise. "I'm so sorry, Avery. He seemed so in love with you."

"Oh, he loves me," Avery says bitterly. "Loving me is why he won't be with me." She looks at me, her expression volatile with hurt and anger. "A girl out at the bayou had a baby two weeks ago," she says. "A little girl. The father is one of Remy's pack." My stomach tenses. I have an idea where this is heading. "She's got the wolf gene," Avery says tightly. "Remy said he could feel it —they all could—the moment she was born. Even if she won't change until adolescence, they can already see her, in their minds, like a shadow on the edge of their sight. They're *aware* of her. Remy says that only happens when someone has the gene, or whatever it is that makes them change." She meets my eyes. "Remy won't take that chance. Especially because of whatever it is that I am. He says we don't know what the result might be. He doesn't want to risk it." She takes a step back, her mouth working painfully. "But you," she says bitterly, "you're a thousand times more powerful than any of us—and you're married to a *vampire*, for goodness' sakes. Remy was worried we might make a dangerous wolf." She laughs, a hard, ugly sound. "Whatever you've got inside you, I'd guarantee it's more dangerous than any wolf I might have birthed. But you'll have it nonetheless, Harper, won't you? And no doubt we'll all end up trying to protect you while you do. Because as usual, it's all about you." She turns away, climbing into her car, but not before I see the tears spill down her cheeks.

"Don't expect congratulations from me," she says thickly. "I don't have them, Harper. All I hope is that whatever is inside you doesn't hurt the people I love, any more than you already have." The wheels of her car churn gravel as she turns, and she passes so close to the gate post on her way out I think for a moment she will hit it. She fishtails onto the road, and her little hatchback gives a protesting squeal as she hits the tarmac. I watch until she is gone.

"Avery didn't take it well, then." I turn to find Callie on the steps, Iara beside her. The newcomer is looking at me with almost the same interest she focused on Avery recently.

"No," I say dully. "She didn't take it well at all."

Iara steps forward, her eyes on my belly. She holds up a hand and glances at me, as if asking permission. I give her a half shrug, and she approaches me, placing her hand on my belly.

I feel a shock of recognition as she does, a queer curling inside my veins that is both thrilling and dark. Iara is the first unknown vampire I have touched since my activation, and I have to force myself to remain still, not to flinch away. Iara's eyes widen as she feels the slow pulse of my blood, and she pulls away as if she's been shocked, staring at my belly in fascination. She glances at Callie. *"Embarazada,"* she whispers, and even my

Spanish is good enough to know she is saying I am pregnant. Callie nods.

In the ensuing silence, Tate and Antoine's raised voices travel through the mansion.

"It's not safe for her to be here!" I can hear the tension in Antoine's voice. "We know nothing about her, Tate. Where she came from, who she is. She could be Keziah's creature for all we know—"

"Keziah killed her Maker, Antoine. Iara has more reason to hate her than any of us. And I won't turn her away."

"You only have her word for that." Antoine's voice is rising as they enter the house. Iara glances toward the voices, and her face crumples in despair. Briefly she grasps my hand. *"Buena suerte."*

"She's wishing you good luck," says Callie needlessly.

Her words come too late, though, for Iara is already gone.

CHAPTER 6

LILIES

"Well done," says Tate sarcastically, turning to Antoine. "A newborn vampire without a Maker or a good command of English, on the loose near a rebel wolf pack. She was already nervous about coming here, embarrassed she was imposing—and now you've scared her off. You seem committed to chaos, brother."

"And you seem committed to trusting any supernatural creature that crosses your path." Antoine scowls at him. "We can't risk Keziah learning of this, Tate."

"Either way, Iara isn't safe on her own." Tate's eyes light on me, and his face softens. He reaches out to hold my hand. His touch is cool and soothing, with none of the erratic thrill I felt in Iara's. It's interesting, I think, how utterly different each being is. "I won't do anything to endanger your child," he says, and his eyes glow with warmth. "I can't imagine a greater miracle than what you carry, Harper. I swear I will do all in my power to keep you both safe."

I cover his hand with my own. "I know that." I meet Antoine's eyes. "He's right. Iara isn't safe out there on her own, nor is anyone else while she's on the run. You need to find her and bring her back."

"Before you go," Callie says, "Jeremiah and I found out some things last night about Iara that you might find interesting." She looks at Tate. Not for the first time, I'm struck by how profoundly Callie's speech has changed since her arrival. I rarely hear the rough Memphis accents now. They seem restricted to when Callie feels uncomfortable, or insecure. "Your friend Ramon must have had some specific idea in mind when he chose her as his progeny," she says. "Iara is from a tribe called the Warao. They live around the Orinoco basin and have a strong relationship with water." She glances at me. "They are also thought to be the origin of the Taíno people in the Caribbean."

"The Taíno? The same people Keziah comes from?"

Callie nods. "Except the Warao have remained largely apart from western civilization, unlike the Taíno, who have long since been dispersed. Most of them don't even speak Spanish. Iara is an exception. Her mother fled their village when Iara was young, after she argued with some kind of shaman in their tribe. I don't understand exactly what happened, only that Iara says her mother was too scared to go back. They ended up in a settlement, where her mother got menial work, and Iara had some very basic schooling."

Antoine turns to Tate. "Did you tell Ramon about what had happened here—Keziah being released?"

"Not in so many words. I didn't want to put anything in writing. I did drop hints, though, and Ramon knew who Keziah was, if not what she was."

"Then perhaps he made Iara with a purpose in mind."

"Perhaps." Tate shoots Antoine a somewhat exasperated look. "And perhaps, if you hadn't frightened Iara so much she ran off, we could ask her ourselves."

"Okay. I'll help you find her." Antoine is watching me, frowning. "I don't want to leave Harper alone."

"I'm fine." I give him a half smile. "You can't supervise me every moment of the next seven and a half months, Antoine."

Antoine doesn't look remotely appeased at this. "Don't leave her side," he says curtly to Jeremiah and Callie. "Not for anything. Do you understand? And call me if anything happens. Anything at all."

I roll my eyes. "I'll be fine." I kiss him. "Go."

Tate gives me a small smile, and they are gone, disappearing into the bright morning sun, gone as quickly as the dawn dew already dry on the grass.

IT'S MIDDAY BEFORE WE HEAR ANYTHING, AND THEN IT IS ONLY A brief text from Antoine to say they've lost Iara's trace and won't be back for a while. I don't receive this message until late afternoon, however. I laid down for a brief moment shortly after Antoine and Tate left, but I must be more tired than I know, because when I wake the shadows are long and I've slept most of the day away.

"Hey, sleepyhead," Callie greets me as I come out onto the back porch. She's seated exactly where I left her, the only difference the stack of books Jeremiah has open by her side. She tells me about Antoine's message. When I look at my own phone I see a dozen missed calls, then a series of texts.

"I answered your phone and told him you were asleep," says Jeremiah. "After that he sent texts instead. But he's called us every hour to check that you're okay."

"He wanted us to wake you up," Callie adds. "But I talked him out of that. I've made you soup, though."

"Thanks." I smile and try to swallow the soup, but I only

really feel thirsty, so I drink pint after pint of water and take a few mouthfuls out of the bowl to make Callie happy. As dusk falls I feel restless. "I'm going to work in the garden for a while," I say, standing up. Callie and Jeremiah exchange a worried glance. "Seriously?" I'm beginning to feel slightly irritated. "It's barely a hundred yards away. You'll see me from where you're sitting."

"Are you sure you should be gardening?" Jeremiah is frowning. "Maybe it's not good for you, all that bending over."

"Oh, for goodness' sake." I go down the stairs, waving him away. "Everyone is going to need to calm down." I pause at the bottom of the steps. "Did Connor come back?" I ask. "Cass?"

Jeremiah shakes his head wordlessly. I turn back and walk down the slope toward the river, finding it hard to think of anything but my brother and my beautiful friend.

My hands in the soil are reassuring, the most real thing I've felt in a while. I glance at the water garden and feel a surge of delight at the water lilies poking above the surface, yet to unfurl. Two grow side by side, their green shoots just above the water but still tightly closed. I touch them affectionately, just letting them know I see them. Somehow it makes me feel better. They look so beautiful, not quite yet born, just like the life inside me. The thought is fanciful but also oddly touching. On an impulse I take a photo of myself in the water beside them, smiling at the thought that one day, I might show this photo to the little miracle inside me and tell her the story. Then I look around guiltily in case someone caught my moment of fancy. Relieved to find nobody watching, I put the phone away again and go back to work.

I lose myself in the familiar sensation of earth and plant, the scent of river water and moonvine, night jasmine opening in the twilight and the tired scent of red magnolias after a hot day. I step into the pond and feel beneath the water for the bulbs growing in the river silt. Other lilies grow in my pond, but they feel different to my two favourite shoots, less exciting. They're still beautiful, though, and I love being among them. I murmur to Tessa as I work, imagining her laughter as if she were beside me. Out of nowhere, I remember her face on one particular day when I came to the hospital, not long before she died. There had been an odd life in it, a strange excitement, as if she could see a future I could not. The memory makes my lips curve and I look around, still smiling, when I hear the rustle of a night bird in the tree behind me.

Except it isn't a night bird.

It's Keziah, standing beneath the branches of the red magnolia, staring straight at me. I'm so shocked it takes a full beat to register it is truly her.

"It's true." Her voice is like cut glass in the still dusk. "You are with child."

I'm frozen with terror, unable to do anything other than stare at her.

Keziah takes a step toward me. "You know that child belongs to me." I can hear the feverish excitement in her voice. She stares at my belly with a fascinated greed that makes my stomach churn. "It's mine by right." Her eyes gleam malevolently. "You took my progeny from me. I wondered how it could happen, but now I know: you took the children of my blood only so that you could give me this one, created of my body."

She takes another step forward and with an effort of will I straighten, my body rigid and stiff, fists clenched as if I can fight her off.

"Harper!" Callie calls my name from the porch, her voice sharp with fear. She flies down the steps and sprints toward me, Jeremiah hard on her heels.

Keziah hisses in excitement. Her arm comes out toward me. Like a slow-motion movie, I know Callie and Jeremiah cannot reach me in time.

Sick terror grips my heart. *I have to protect my babies.* The thought is all there is, an impulse so visceral it takes over everything else. I know I can't outrun Keziah. But I feel a strange tugging from within, as if something is calling me to safety, and the supernatural senses within me tell me to trust it.

I close my eyes.

And then I'm spinning into darkness, tumbling on the indigo sea toward something that is drawing me inexorably forward, though it keeps me blinded and confused. I come to a sudden halt, my body feeling battered and bruised, aware that I am no longer in darkness.

I open my eyes.

CHAPTER 7

FOUNTAIN

I'm still knee-deep in water. But it smells of chlorine rather than of mud, and instead of night shadows, the sun blazes high overhead.

People are staring at me. A small girl holding her mother's hand points at me and giggles. I look down. There are coins gleaming underwater on the turquoise tiles. I'm standing in a fountain. I stare at the coins dumbly and realize my fists are still tightly clenched, and that in one of them I hold a water lily from my garden. I clutch it close as I clamber out of the fountain, trying to ignore the sideways glances and disapproving muttering of people passing by. I notice several people dressed in blue scrubs. There must be a hospital nearby. Then I catch sight of a young man who looks vaguely familiar. It takes me a moment to place him, and when I do, I frown.

It's Max, a nurse from the hospital in Baton Rouge whom I met when Tessa was sick. He was incredibly kind to Connor and me during the final days of Tessa's illness. The only problem is, I know for a fact that Max is no longer in the US. He and Connor are friends on social media, and as of yesterday,

Max was somewhere in Eastern Europe, drinking cheap beer and asking advice on the cheapest route to Moscow.

I turn around slowly.

I'm standing in the middle of the Mall of Louisiana in Baton Rouge. I know the place exactly. It's barely a ten minutes' walk from Baton Rouge General Hospital. When Tessa was sick, I came here almost every day, sitting by the fountain while I ate something that wasn't hospital food.

Because I don't know what else to do, I start walking toward the hospital. I'm still clutching the lily in one hand. It feels like the only thing linking me to reality. My legs dry as I walk, and by the time I go through the sliding doors, I no longer look like I just stepped out of a fountain. Behind the counter, I see a nurse I used to greet every day. She looks exactly like I remember her.

Exactly like I remember her.

Down to the plastic pair of earrings shaped like bunches of grapes that her four-year-old daughter had insisted she wear to work—and which had broken off in the early evening one day and been thrown into the cafeteria trash, alongside the paper cup into which I'd shed tears as she comforted me.

I swallow hard.

Instinctively, I duck into a nearby corridor to avoid her gaze, then take an elevator, pushing buttons without thinking. It's only when the doors open in front of me that I recognize the floor and realize I'm heading for Tessa's room. My feet falter for a moment.

This is insane. *I'm* insane. A moment ago, I was standing in the water garden facing down Keziah, more terrified than I can recall ever feeling in my life. Now I'm somehow in Baton Rouge. In the hospital where my sister took her last breath. And if my scrambled brain is making any sense, I'm here days before Tessa actually died.

Callie's words from earlier ring in my mind: *We've gotten used to weird.*

There's weird, I think, *and then there's whatever this is.* Weird doesn't begin to cover what is happening right now. I half expect to wake and find Antoine leaning over me, laughing at my strange dreams.

I'm outside Tessa's room. I spent so much time behind that door that I'd know it anywhere. I trod the route to this room so often I thought I'd wear a path in the glossy, sterile hospital floor.

I take a deep breath and push it open. Then the world stops.

Tessa is lying in bed.

Miraculously, incredibly, alive.

I freeze, just staring at the impossible sight of my sister, unsure if I want to cry, scream, or embrace her.

Her eyes are closed. She is as pale as I remember her being during her final days, the skin of her eyelids almost transluscent. She's so still I'm afraid all over again that she has stopped breathing, until I realize that it's me holding my breath. I let it out in an audible rush.

Tessa's eyelids fly open. Her head turns weakly toward me. Her eyes flare slightly, and her mouth curves in a wondering smile. I can't move. I can barely breathe.

"Harper," she says, and one pale hand raises slightly off the coverlet, extending toward me. "You came, just like you said you would."

"Tessa." My mouth is dry, the word no more than a cracked whisper. I try to walk toward the bed and stumble, tripping over my own feet, my eyes locked on the pale figure that for so long has been nothing more than a memory, a whisper on the wind. "Tessa," I croak, tears spilling down my face. "It's you. It's really you."

"Yes." She smiles weakly.

I reach out and grasp her hand, almost leaping back when I feel her material form, my beautiful sister whom I have missed every day since she drew her last breath. Her eyes are the brilliant green I remember. "They aren't the same as mine," I whisper, staring at her. "I kept looking in the mirror, Tessa, because I thought our eyes were the same and that if I looked long enough, I'd see you in my own. But they're different. I don't know how, but they are."

I know I make no sense. But there is no sense to be made, and I don't know what to say. Tessa's hand covers my own, and when I look up, I see tears glistening in my twin's eyes as well. "It's okay, Harper," she says gently. "You explained it all to me yesterday. I know how strange this must seem to you, but believe me, it isn't as strange as you might think. I've just had longer to get used to it than you."

"Yesterday?" I stare at her. "What do you mean, yesterday?"

"You came then, too, and you gave me things to give to you today. Open the drawer." She nods at the bedside table, then her hand on mine tightens at the sound of voices in the corridor. "Hurry," she says, pressing my fingers. "We don't have much time."

Too bemused to argue, I open the drawer. "The jar," Tessa says. I lift it out. It's a jar I recognize, from my own kitchen—in the Marigny mansion.

A mansion that was no more than a plan on a page when Tessa was still alive and here, in hospital.

"It's impossible," I breathe, staring at the jar.

"You have to drink it," Tessa says. I hear the urgency in her voice and turn back to her. "It's from your garden," Tessa says. "You're not sure if it's that or the lily in your hand that helps get you back. They said you should drink it anyway."

"'They'?" I repeat blankly, staring at her. "Who's 'they,' Tessa?"

"The twins." Tessa nods at the drawer. "And they said you need to take those with you, Harper." I look down into the drawer and see two small, teardrop glass pendants: bottles with tiny corks in the top. They're sealed with what looks like wax and protected by filigree silver.

"Is that blood?" I stare at the rosy liquid barely visible through the delicate silver design.

"We think so, yes." Tessa's hand tightens on mine again. "Your blood, Harper—and Antoine's."

"Antoine's?" My heart stops beating for a moment then starts again, a slow, steady thudding. "Twins, Tessa?"

My sister glances down at my belly, and her mouth curves in a soft, sad smile that breaks my heart into a thousand pieces and makes me sink onto the bed and clutch both her hands in my own. "How is this possible?" I say roughly. "Is it a dream? A vision? Am I dead?"

"You're not dead, Harper." Tessa holds my eyes, then the phone on the pillow beside her dings, and her eyes widen. "But you do have to hurry," she says. "That's Connor texting to say you and he are only five minutes away. You have to be gone before he arrives, Harper. You can't be seen by anyone—and you can't see yourself. It's one of the laws."

"There are laws?"

"Listen to me, Harper." Tessa grips my hands with unusual strength for someone so ill. "Your twins are able to travel through time, but they need water to do it, and to be able to get back, they need those pendants in your hand. Never let those pendants go so long as you're pregnant, Harper. And after they are born, make sure your girls never, ever take them off. That's the only way they can find their way back to you, do you understand? You must make certain you have them." She looks at my denim shorts. "You have your phone, don't you?" I reach into my pocket and pull it out, nodding. "There's a photo on there," Tessa says. "Of you, in the garden. When you go back to the fountain, you need to hold that photo close to your belly. Look at it yourself, then hold it close to your bare skin. Make sure you have the lily with you. And drink what is in that jar. Everything in it comes from your garden, on that same day, including the water. It will be enough to help the twins get you home."

"But—" I pause at the sound of Connor's voice, low and strained, at the end of the corridor.

"You can't be seen." Tessa half raises herself off the pillows in her agitation. "You have to go, Harper. Do you hear me? You have to go now."

"How?" I stare at her. "How are you so sure this will work?"

Tessa smiles again, the same sadness still darkening her beautiful emerald eyes. "Because you told me it does," she says softly. "Now go, Harper. Trust me —and go."

I let go of her hand and go to the door. It's still clear; I can hear Connor at the nurses' station around the corner. I glance back at Tessa once. "Go," she mouths. I stumble down the corridor, her touch still tingling on my skin, resisting the urge to look behind me. I can hear Connor's footsteps coming closer. I round the corner and take the back stairs, my footsteps echoing in the empty stairwell. I push open the heavy security door and emerge into the blazing afternoon, barely aware of my surroundings. I keep my head down and wish I could disappear as easily as I'd come. I'm terrified of being seen. I'm terrified of being here. Most of all, I'm terrified to leave Tessa behind, when I've only just found her again.

"You explained it all to me yesterday."

That means I come back, I think as I hurry toward the mall. *It makes no sense, but if I was with Tessa yesterday, then somehow I come back.* My hand closes hard on the jar and lily, the other touching the pendants in my denim pocket. *And I bring these things with me.*

Right now though, all I can think of is trying to get back— and what is waiting for me when I do. I shudder. What will I do about Keziah? How will I fight her off? I look at the jar in my hand. *I come back.* Somehow, I come back. Which means I must find a way to deal with Keziah when I return today.

I glance over my shoulder, just in time to see Max wandering back through the mall. He looks up, squinting in the sun as he stares at me, frowning in confusion. I'd seen him in the parking lot that day, I remember. We had a chat about his plans to travel as soon as the semester was finished.

I need to get out of here. Right now.

I unscrew the lid on the jar and gulp the green liquid inside. It tastes sweet and grassy and smells so much like my garden my heart twists. I step clumsily into the fountain, ignoring the startled glances of passersby. Pulling out my phone, I find the picture that Connor took of me yesterday, in the garden, before I told anyone I was pregnant. I stare at it, remembering the way the air felt on my skin, the way I felt in that moment, hugging my miracle to myself. I pick up my T-shirt and press the screen against my belly with one hand, clutching the lily with the other. "Take us home," I whisper aloud, staring down at my belly. "Take us back to the water garden."

For a terrible moment nothing happens, and my heart lurches in fear and confusion.

Then something stirs inside me. As if I'm somehow disintegrating, pieces of me swirl into chaos, gaining speed, spinning into the darkness, until I am lost again on the indigo sea, tumbling into nothingness. Then the air grows dense, the particles seeming to coalesce, until finally with a thud, I feel the earth, solid and wet beneath me.

I'm standing in the water garden at the back of the mansion, holding my phone against my belly.

A breeze touches my face. I remember yesterday, the way I thought I heard Tessa's voice whisper to me on the breeze.

"Are you truly here, Tessa?" I spin on the spot, looking about wildly. Maybe she is. Maybe I haven't been imagining my sister this entire time. *It's possible,* I think, my head spinning. *Tessa could be here. She could be still alive, somehow.* I walk over to the trees and stand under their shelter, staring into the woods, wondering if it is possible that Tessa is there, somewhere. But I can't see her, and despite whispering her name a few more times, the only answer I get is the breeze. "It's me," I say quietly. "Harper." Something seems wrong, off somehow, though I can't imagine what it is.

A moment later, Antoine's boat pulls up at the jetty, and he leaps out in a fluid movement as Jeremiah throws him the rope. My heart leaps, and I open my mouth to cry out, then close it again just as quickly as I see the expression on his face.

I remember that expression.

It was the one he wore when he asked me if Tate was here.

A terrible sense of foreboding grips me. I shrink into the trees, ruffled by that same familiar breeze.

It's yesterday, I think wildly.

Before Iara. Before Keziah. Before anyone knows that I'm pregnant.

I've come back to the wrong day.

CHAPTER 8

WATER

I press myself back into the trees, my heart pounding, and look at the jar I'm still clutching in my hand. There's a little liquid still left in it. The lily is still in my other hand, though it is wilting fast. I turn back to the garden. Antoine and Jeremiah are walking toward the mansion. For some reason I'm not there, even though I was, in my memory of this moment. Perhaps, I think, I had it wrong.

It's the strangest thing I can imagine, the thought of actually seeing myself. I shiver and turn away.

Quickly, I try to remember the events of the previous day. The sound of Tate's truck triggers my memories. *They are all inside,* I think, *meeting Iara.*

I have a few moments.

Glancing about nervously, I step out of the trees and move over to the pond. The lilies have yet to break the surface. I hadn't noticed that a moment ago. With shaking hands, I scroll through my photos, finding the one I'd taken just before Keziah arrived, of the two lilies showing above the water, me standing among them. I hold it up and fix it in my mind, then put it in front of my belly again. "I'm so sorry," I whisper. "I'm so sorry to make you do this again. But I can't be here. I have to go back to this day, this moment. Can you take me there?" I pause for a moment, then add: "Not exactly to the same spot, okay? Put me in the river you can see in this photo, behind the pond. Near the red magnolia. Can you do that, my beautiful miracles? Can you take Mommy to that spot?"

I know how crazy it is. I know they can't possibly understand. But I don't know what else to do. I raise the jar. "Please work," I whisper. "Please, please work."

I step into the pond, and close my eyes, fear flooding every cell of my body.

This time, the darkness rushes to meet me, sucking me into the void with disquieting force, as if I'm being tugged and pushed at the same time. I smack into consciousness far quicker than before, feeling the river mud between my toes before my eyes even open. Then I am standing in the river, staring at Keziah's tall, straight back, barely a dozen paces away. Beyond her, I know, is me, hidden from my sight by Keziah's body.

"Harper!" I hear Callie cry as she leaps from the porch. Keziah hisses and takes a step toward the other, earlier me, then stops, startled. The earlier me has disappeared.

Keziah screams, a high-pitched sound of frustration, and under cover of the noise, I sink into the water and swim quietly into the cypress roots lining the bank. From their shelter, I watch as Keziah stares around in confusion then leaves, as rapidly as she came, flying across the water toward Louisiana. She passes so close I feel the rush of air as she goes, and for a terrible moment I think she senses me, for her head seems to turn my way; but as she does, Antoine's warning shout cuts the air.

Keziah lands on the opposite shore and is gone.

"Harper!" Antoine is standing on the edge of the water, his face horrified. "Where did she go?" He turns on Callie, grasping her shoulders so hard she winces.

"I don't know!" Callie's voice catches. "She was here. I swear she was, Antoine. Then Keziah came, and Harper just . . . disappeared."

"What do you mean, she disappeared? Did Keziah take her?"

I'm trying to clamber out of the water, but the bank is steep and muddy, the roots slippery to the touch. "I'm here," I try to say, but neither figure turns.

"Jeremiah!" Antoine roars, letting Callie go. "Jeremiah! Harper's gone!" He swings around to look over the river, and his eyes glow a dark, dangerous red, a color as strange to me as the wild, furious note in his voice.

"Antoine," I gasp, hauling myself up onto the bank. "I'm here. Over here." I'm barely whispering, but it's enough to reach supernatural ears, for as soon as I've spoken, Antoine is at my side, pulling me to my feet and into his arms, utterly unheeding of my mud-soaked body.

"Thank God," he murmurs, over and over. "Thank God, Harper. I thought you were gone. I thought she'd taken you."

For a long time, I don't want to be anywhere else but right here, Antoine's arms around me, one large hand cradling my head against him, his lips murmuring against my hair, the wild beat of our hearts gradually slowing until we can both breathe again.

When I step back, Callie is staring at me in confusion. "You disappeared," she says bluntly. "I was running toward you. Keziah was reaching for you, and I knew I'd be too late, that she would take you. And then you were just gone. Gone, Harper. I saw it with my own eyes."

"I know," I say, trying to keep my voice steady. "It's okay, Callie. I know what you saw. You aren't crazy." I take a shaky breath and try for a reassuring smile, though by the looks on Antoine, Jeremiah, and Callie's faces, I fall sadly short. "Or at least, not unless I'm crazy, too. Which you may well think I am, after I tell you what happened. I'm still not sure I believe it myself."

"So long as you and our baby are safe," says Antoine, "and here with me, I'll believe anything you tell me."

"Not one baby." I cover my belly with my hand and smile through the tears threatening to spill from my eyes. "Two, Antoine. Twins."

He stares at me, frowning in confusion. "Twins," he repeats flatly. "Did you have a home visit from your doctor in the hour since I left?"

"Not quite. Although I did go to a hospital." At Callie's bemused expression, I shake my head. "I'm not doing this very well," I mutter, trying to collect my scattered thoughts. "I don't know where to even start."

"Why don't we get you cleaned up," says Antoine gently, taking my arm and leading me toward the mansion, "and you can start right at the beginning."

I nod, but as we go up the stairs, I shrink into his side, suddenly unwilling to be on my own. Reality feels too fragile, too uncertain. "You know, I think I'd rather just tell you now. If I could just have some water—"

I sit down as multiple containers of water are pushed at me. I drink them all. I can't remember ever having felt this thirsty, and the thought gives me a savage thrust of guilt. What if traveling like this is hurting my babies? Tessa told me they use water to travel through time, just as my own magic works in water. What if this thirst is actually theirs, exhaustion from the effort of moving not only their own tiny, barely material forms, but mine as well?

"I'm sorry," I gasp, tears falling down my cheeks as I clutch my belly. "I'm so, so sorry."

"Harper!" Antoine squats before me, my hands in his own, his face drawn with worry. "Why on earth are you sorry? What is it?"

I shake my head, battling the emotions that keep surging in me, the tears I can't seem to make stop.

"The twins," I say. "They can time travel, Antoine."

For a moment there is dead silence, and then I see Callie and Jeremiah exchange a look behind Antoine's back and the sudden, dark concern clouding Antoine's eyes. "Time travel," he repeats blankly.

"I know it sounds crazy." When nobody says anything, I take another breath, forcing myself to steady this time, the tears to recede. I press Antoine's hands in my own. "Please," I say quietly. "You need to listen to me, Antoine."

Listen to me, Harper . . .

I blink, shutting out my sister's voice, forcing myself to focus on the present. I look at each of them in turn.

"I was standing in the water garden," I begin.

CHAPTER 9

RETURN

Somewhere in the middle of my story, Antoine lets go of my hands. I'm not certain when he begins edging away from me, but by the time I finish, he is leaning against the door-frame, arms folded, as remote as if he were in a separate land.

"And now you're saying you want to go back." His voice is carefully neutral and his face gives nothing away, but I can feel the tension emanating from him.

"It's not that I *want* to go back." I don't know how to make him understand. "I have to. If I don't, Tessa won't be able to give me the pendants, or the jar." I pause and look around at their skeptical faces. "You don't believe me."

"You have to admit," says Jeremiah, glancing awkwardly at Antoine, "it's a little out there, Harper."

"More out there than ancient vampires trapped in our cellar by a curse? Or humans who turn into wolves?" I hold his eyes. "After everything we've seen, Jeremiah, is it really such a stretch to learn that time travel is real?"

"No." Antoine pushes off from the door and sits beside me again. He smiles crookedly, the greatest comfort I can possibly imagine at that moment. "But in almost three centuries, I've only ever heard of it once—and that was nothing more than a wild story, a rumor during a time of war, when men are inclined to believe things they wouldn't otherwise."

"Then you don't believe me." It hurts more than I could possibly have imagined. Amid the chaos of first traveling, then meeting Tessa, then trying to get back, it never occurred to me that my story wouldn't be believed.

Especially by Antoine.

"I didn't say that," he says gently. "But I do need to ask, Harper—is there any chance, any at all, that this could somehow have been a dream, or something planted, perhaps, in your mind?"

I shake my head silently. I don't trust myself to speak. My distress must show, because a moment later Antoine is at my side, his arm about me protectively. "Okay, Harper. I'm sorry I asked. Maybe you should have that shower, get some of the mud off, and we can talk about what we should do."

"I've already told you what I need to do." I stand up angrily, shrugging off his arm. "I need to go back, Antoine. If I don't, I won't know any of this. We may never have this conversation. And I won't have these." I pull the pendants out of my pocket and place them on the table, where they glow beneath the porch light with what seems like an inner fire. I'd left them until last, hoping, I guess, that my story would be enough. But Tessa told me I had been with her the day before, and so I know I will return. And besides, the alternative is too terrible to contemplate. If I don't return and talk with Tessa, I won't have the means to escape. I can't risk being lost there, in that time, living all those years again. And who is to say that I would still meet Antoine? What would happen, if I got lost in time? What would happen to our beautiful babies? I shudder, unable to bear so much as thinking about it.

"What are they?" Jeremiah leans in close, fascinated by the pendants.

"They're anchors, I guess." I frown. "I'm not sure exactly how they work. Tessa said she thinks they are made with Antoine's and my blood. She told me I must keep them with me while I'm pregnant—and that after the twins are born, they must wear them, always, so they can find their way back to us."

"I believe you." It's Callie who speaks. I look at her gratefully. "You do?"

She nods. "I saw you disappear, Harper. Right in front of my eyes." She meets Antoine's eyes, then Jeremiah's. "You didn't see what I did. One moment she was right there, so close I could almost touch her. Then she was just—gone. And it wasn't just me. Keziah saw it, too. It frightened her. She didn't understand it at all. Whatever this time travel thing is, I'd swear she's never seen it, either."

"Thank you." I grip her hand gratefully. "Thank you so much."

"It's not that I don't believe you." Antoine is frowning. "If you say you went through time, Harper, then that is what happened. But I've lived through Keziah's mind control. I know the power she has. I've believed things I could never have imagined I could believe, seen visions more extraordinary than you can imagine, and thought them real. My own experiences are all I have to go by. These, though,"—he lifts up the pendants and weighs them in his palm, his face thoughtful—"you're right, these are something else altogether. But if you take them back through time with you, then how will you travel back here again? It makes no sense. And why isn't your twin certain of what is inside them? Until we understand more of how all this works, there's no way you're going back."

"Then you do believe me." I'm almost weak with relief.

"I believe you." He gives me a small smile that doesn't dispel the grave look in his eyes. "But I think it is better if we keep this strictly amongst ourselves, for now. I don't want anyone knowing. Not even Tate, for now. Not until I've had a chance to try to find out what is going on." He looks directly at Jeremiah and Callie. "Is that understood?"

They nod. "Of course," says Jeremiah. "Although Tate might be our best bet to find out what is going on."

"Tate has a newborn vampire to look after," Antoine says. "We found Iara just before I came back. She was in quite a state, disoriented, upset. I still don't trust her. I don't want even the slightest risk that she may find out about this. For now, nobody knows. Nobody. Not even your brother, Harper."

I shake my head. "I wouldn't know what to tell him, anyway," I say quietly. "Speaking of Tessa would only hurt him, dig up old wounds he's barely managed to heal. I don't want to tell him. He has enough to cope with as it is." I stare at the pendants on the table. "If they're already made, then where did they come from? Who made them?"

Antoine frowns. "I don't know. I don't understand any of this." He rakes his hands through his hair, and I realize how frustrated he is. It almost makes me smile. For a vampire who has lived as long as he has, there must be few mysteries left.

He looks up and catches me smiling. "You finding something amusing in this?"

I shrug. "Only the fact that for the first time since we met, I've experienced something that you haven't. I can't say I'm not enjoying the novelty."

We talk for a while longer, but it's as if the more we discuss the strange events of the day, the more they disappear, becoming blurred and confused. I'm suddenly exhausted, my body aching as if I've run a marathon. "I'm going to bed." I touch Antoine's arm and shake my head when he rises to come with me. "Stay. I'll be asleep in moments." It isn't that I don't want him with me. I just feel the need to try to organize my thoughts a little, make sense of the experience in my own mind, rather than listening to the speculation of others. I can feel Antoine's eyes on my back as I leave the room. His concern is palpable. I know he is uneasy about leaving me alone. He doesn't try to stop me, though, for which I'm grateful.

After my shower, I sit on the bed wrapped in a towel. I know I should lie down, but somehow my body doesn't seem to be my own anymore. It takes a moment for my tired mind to register that I'm staring directly at the framed photo of Tessa that sits on my bedside table.

My heart jolts, a tired, jagged beat that catches at my throat. It is incomprehensible that Tessa is dead when I saw her only hours ago, touched her hand. A savage rush of grief and longing makes my heart clench again. *I have to go back,* I think fiercely. *You said I did, and I will.* I pick up the photo, staring at my sister's beautiful eyes. I remember the day I took the picture. I'd skipped my last class and gone to the hospital instead, unwilling to miss a moment of what some part of me knew were Tessa's final days. She'd been oddly animated that day, a hint of color in her cheeks, and she'd asked me to take her picture. "This is how I want you to remember me," she'd said, impatiently brushing away my protests that she'd be fine. "We both know I'm never coming home, Harper. But at least you'll have one photograph of me smiling, instead of sick in bed. Print the photo out and put it by your bed. Promise me."

I smile at the memory. It was so unusual for Tessa to even allow me to photograph her that I'd done what she asked, and when the next day she wanted to see proof, I'd gone and had the photo printed off and put in a frame, just to ease her mind. "You'll keep it?" she'd asked, gripping my hands when I showed her. "Always, Harper. By your bed. Promise."

And I had. I'd kept the photo close by me, on my nightstand no matter where I slept. When we'd come to the mansion, Tessa's photo was the first thing I'd unpacked, sleeping with it on the floor beside me back when we had no power and my bed was a blow-up mattress on dirty floorboards. Tears prick my eyes as I brush my thumbs over the image. Less than a week after I took it, Tessa died. Looking at her smiling face, her death is as incomprehensible now as it was to me then.

Then.

My thumbs still on the frame. I stare at my sister's face. "It was that day." My voice is oddly loud in the stillness. "The day you asked me to take your photograph—it was the day before the one I traveled to. I remember now. That's why Connor and I were late getting to the hospital the next day. I'd gone to get your photo printed off and framed, to show you."

That's why she asked me to take her photo. I know it, deep inside. *She'd already seen me that day. That's why she was so happy and excited. She knew I would need this photograph to get back to her, to that day. It's why she made me promise to keep the photo with me always.*

I already know the photos help me go where, and when, I need to. This photograph of Tessa is my pathway back to that day, the day before Keziah triggered my first time travel. I can use the photograph to get back to Tessa.

And the potion. Tessa said it might help me come back. And even if it had taken me to the wrong day, I feel as if it did help. The taste and scent of the plants in the drink had felt like home, somehow. Hastily, I pull my clothes on again and slip silently out of the back door, ignoring the low murmured conversation coming from the salon. I pick the edible flowers and herbs that grow in both my night garden and the water garden. I've still got the mortar and pestle I used to make Connor's potion up in my room. And in the bathroom there is a drum Connor rigged up to capture rainwater in case our water failed again. I can use some of that.

I mix the drink in the jar Tessa gave me, without rinsing it out. Perhaps whatever is left in there has a magic of its own that will help me get back.

But then what? I glance at the pendants again. I took them with me when I came upstairs, despite Antoine's worried frown. I'm keeping them with me, just as Tessa told me to.

As I fall into sleep, though, I can't help but think that Antoine was right—if I take the pendants and potion to Tessa, how will I get back myself?

CHAPTER 10

WARAO

I sleep almost an entire day and wake feeling refreshed and clear, although my body feels bruised still, as if I've done a heavy day at the gym. The sun is midmorning high, and the day smells of summer. I lie in my bedroom peace for a time, my hands on my belly, imagining the little beings inside. I mentally remind myself to make an appointment for an ultrasound. Antoine made me promise that he could be with me when I have it. Although he wasn't explicit, I know he wants to be there in case the ultrasound shows something abnormal. Something that might require a swift compulsion of the attending doctor.

Something with fangs, for example.

I make an appointment for the following day while I'm lying there, feeling a sense of unreality as the confirmation message shows on my phone.

Voices drift up from the back porch. I make out Tate and Antoine's and feel reassured when I hear the hesitant sounds of Iara's Spanish. I'm glad she's here. When I hear Jeremiah and Callie arrive, I figure I should probably get up.

I don't hear Cass or Connor. I try not to think about that.

When I come downstairs, I find a platter of cut fruit and croissants waiting. *"Pero no cafe,"* Iara says, waving a finger remonstratively when I reach for the coffee pot. She points at my belly. *"No es buena para las bebés."*

Antoine stiffens, his face darkening. I shoot him a warning glance, and he makes an effort to smooth his expression before Iara sees it. I know he is uneasy about her knowing anything about this pregnancy, even the fact that I'm having twins, but I don't want to do anything to scare her off again, and despite his misgivings, neither does Antoine. A newborn vampire is much safer in my house, surrounded by the more powerful of her kind, than running loose, a target for Keziah.

"So, Iara." I smile at her. "Is it okay if I ask Callie to translate for me?"

Tate stiffens. "Harper, I haven't had a chance to ask her anything yet—"

"Then there's no time like the present." I'm not really in the mood for Tate's careful diplomacy. If Iara is any kind of threat, it's better that we know as much about her as possible. Secrets, in my experience, have done little but cause problems. I remember belatedly that I'm still keeping the most explosive secret at all. Tate and Iara know nothing of my recent trip to the past. I have to remember to give nothing of it away.

"Tate told us you come from Venezuela, from a tribe called the Warao?"

Callie repeats my question in rapid Spanish, and Iara glances at Tate for reassurance. When he shrugs, albeit grudgingly, she returns my smile tentatively and nods. *"Si."* Iara glances at Callie and says something I don't understand.

"She's surprised you've heard of her people," Callie says. "They are very isolated and often don't even speak Spanish, so few people know much about them."

"How is it that she learned to speak Spanish?" I ask.

Iara doesn't wait for Callie to translate but bursts into a

voluble torrent of Spanish, amid which I can discern some English words also. "Iara says that she had already learned Spanish because her mother fled their village when Iara was younger. Her mother was important among their people, though I don't understand the word she is using to describe her." Callie looks at Iara. "Hoarotu?" She tries out the word, and Iara nods eagerly. "It's some kind of shaman, I think," Callie says, frowning as she tries to decipher Iara's rapid Spanish. "They have different types of shaman for different types of sickness. Iara's mother was the shaman who healed the problems of animals and plants. Her father died several years ago, which is when they fled. He also was a shaman, but a different type. A—wisiratu, I think she is calling it." Callie listens for a moment and her eyes widen. "The wisiratu is the most powerful shaman of the entire tribe," she says slowly. "They preside over the village's house of worship, where the tribe keep the—" Callie shakes her head. "I don't understand what she means."

"Wait." Jeremiah is leaning forward, hands clasped between his knees, staring at Iara in fascination. "She's talking about the kanobotuma." Iara's eyes widen and she nods frantically, staring at Jeremiah as she continues her rapid speech, but now it is Jeremiah who is talking. "I read about them when I researched the Warao. The kanobotuma are wooden or stone icons," Jeremiah says. "They depict the Warao gods and are kept in the temple. The wisiratu shaman is the mediator between the icons and the tribe, interpreting their will and enlisting their help to cure the most deadly sicknesses. He is a very powerful healer and spends a lot of his time in the spirit realm."

"I'm not going to ask why you know all this." Callie shoots Jeremiah a wry grin. "But your nerdiness serves some purpose. What you're saying is more or less what Iara is telling me."

"If her parents were so powerful, why did she and her mother flee?" Tate asks. "She hasn't told me. Maybe she will tell you."

Callie asks the question. Iara's face tightens, her eyes flashing with enough preternatural savagery to remind me of what lies beneath the sweet, vulnerable surface. "The shamans of her tribe were threatened by Iara," Callie says. "It isn't customary for the shamans to have children together." She frowns, concentrating, then holds up a hand to slow the torrent of words and translates in a rush: "Iara was the child of a very powerful union, and some in the tribe saw her as a threat. She also showed promise in the art of healing from a young age. After Iara's father died, a series of"—she frowns and asks a question—"I think she means suspicious accidents, made her mother fear that if they stayed, Iara would never survive to adulthood. Iara's mother made the difficult decision to flee the river village for one of the settlements on the outskirts of the forest. They spent several years there, which is where Iara learned Spanish. Her mother made a small living making traditional medicines for others of the Warao who live there. It was there that Ramon found her."

"But why?" Tate is smiling reassuringly at Iara, but he is as confused as the rest of us. "Why would Ramon have been there —and why would he have chosen to make Iara a vampire?"

Iara answers without waiting for Callie or Tate to translate, so they both give us pieces of the next part of the story. Iara's smile has faded, her voice hard and angry.

"Another shaman from their village sent people to find Iara and her mother," Callie says. "This shaman was called—"

"*Bahanarotu,* I think she says," Tate takes up the story. "He was the shaman who healed material wounds, made by"—he pauses, while Iara rattles a quick torrent of Spanish—"foreign objects, I think. It seems that even far away, this bahanarotu worried they would prove a threat to his power in the temple. The men he sent came in the night and killed Iara's mother. Iara fled into the forest and hid for several days, alone and afraid. That was when Ramon found her. He offered her the chance for revenge on the men who had killed her mother—and on the shaman who had ordered it.

"That figures." Tate is nodding. "Ramon was a warrior, a fierce one. He never told me the details of his background, but I know he originally came from a South American tribe. For many centuries he was a ruthless killer. By the time I met him he had mellowed somewhat, but even during the Napoleonic wars he was a mercenary and a spy. He did love war. It doesn't surprise me that he offered her revenge."

"You think that is all it was?" Antoine looks skeptical. "Didn't you say the Warao are thought to be ancestors of the Taíno, Jeremiah?"

Callie turns to Iara and translates the question. Iara shrugs. "She doesn't know anything about the Taíno," Callie says. "All she knows is that Ramon helped her take revenge on the men who killed her mother." Her mouth twists in a small smile. "Apparently her first kill was the shaman himself."

Iara's eyes glitter savagely, and I find myself wondering what the shaman thought, when he saw the red-eyed monster his own jealousy had unleashed.

"That's more or less the story," Tate says. "They came straight from there to here. Ramon told her they were going to make a new life here. And then Keziah came, and Ramon was dead—which is when you found her." Iara reaches out and clasps Tate's hand gratefully, her eyes shining. "She says she thought Tate was an angel when he rescued her," Callie says, and for the first time since I've known him, Tate looks decidedly uncomfortable. He pats her hand awkwardly and studiously ignores Antoine's somewhat amused expression.

"An angel," Antoine says dryly. "A good thing she didn't know you in your earlier years, brother."

"I told her about them." Tate has visibly colored beneath his natural ruddy bronze, but he meets Antoine's eyes squarely nonetheless. "I had to. Iara's Maker was Ramon, don't forget, and her first kill was just as savage, by all accounts. She is the daughter of two of the most powerful in her tribe, and now she has gone from being a quiet schoolgirl learning Spanish in a remote backwater to the progeny of an ancient, savage killer. Her personality has been transformed by the evil bahanarotu she took as her first kill. She is battling urges that rival any we ourselves faced. She needs all the help we can offer."

"And maybe she can offer us help." I turn to Antoine, feeling a surge of hope. "Maybe she could help me make . . ." my voice trails off as I see the forbidding warning in Antoine's eyes, the brief shake of his head that warns me not to say anything more. "Maybe she knows things that could help me make the garden better," I finish lamely. "Since her mother worked with plants."

"I don't think its a good idea for you to be alone together," Antoine says abruptly. "Not until we know more about her, at least."

I know he's afraid. I am, too. But I'm even more afraid that I will fail to return to Tessa. Now, though, is not the time to argue.

We pass a peaceful enough day, and eat together that evening, Jeremiah asking Iara endless questions about the Warao and their customs, until Tate laughingly tells him he will have enough to write a dissertation before even beginning his studies. I sit on the back porch and watch the moon rise, my hand resting on my belly, marveling at the secrets I hold within.

CHAPTER 11

SHADOWS

I wake on the day of the ultrasound to find Antoine lying fully clothed beside me, hands interlaced under his head and legs crossed at the ankle, frowning fixedly at the ceiling.

"Good morning." I curl into his side and he pulls me close with one arm, kissing the top of my head. I'm not fooled. "You're worried."

His arm tightens briefly. "Aren't you?"

"No." My hand curls into his neck and I press closer to him. "I can feel them inside me, Antoine. Maybe it's hormones, or just crazy optimism, but I'm not worried at all. At least," I amend, thinking of Keziah, "not about the twins." His arm tightens about me again.

"But that's just it." His chest rumbles comfortingly under my cheek. "Even if you're right, and everything is normal, that's only the beginning. There's so much out there that can hurt you."

"But I have you." I reach up to kiss him, enjoying his sharp intake of breath. "And we have friends who will help us. That's

65

more than many women have, Antoine. I don't feel afraid. I feel lucky."

"Lucky." He shakes his head, but he is half smiling. "Only you could think of this—any of this—as lucky."

"Well, I do." I'm about to roll out of bed when he kisses me again. Then I seem to forget about getting up, and in the end we miss breakfast in our rush to make the appointment.

"WELL, YOU HAVE THE TIMING RIGHT." DR. CARTER IS IN HER midforties and a relative newcomer to Deepwater, which explains the warm congratulations and total lack of judgment in her face as she smiles at me. She glances at the screen. "Eight weeks is exactly where you are. Although I'm fascinated by how you knew you were having twins." She glances between Antoine and me, her smile deepening to one of amusement as she takes in Antoine's shell-shocked expression. "I take it you weren't both so sure," she says, giving me a conspiratorial wink.

"My husband thought I was being superstitious," I say hastily. "I have a friend who plays around with crystals and things. It was a lucky guess, I suppose. We were just having fun." I return her smile, mentally cursing the slip when I first came in, referring to the babies in the plural rather than singular.

"Well, maybe your friend is more talented than you think." Dr. Carter smiles again and turns to Antoine, who still hasn't spoken. He's staring at the screen as if he's carved in stone, eyes locked on the two tiny shapes. I can almost see his preternatural hearing splitting the rapid drumming into two distinct heartbeats. "It's a lot to take in," the doctor says tactfully.

Antoine turns to her, his face particularly intent, and my own heart skips a beat as I see her eyes become unfocused and distant when he speaks in a low voice. "Do you see anything in this ultrasound that would cause you concern? Anything even the slightest bit unusual? Tell the truth."

"I see two perfectly normal fetuses," says Dr. Carter instantly. "I see nothing unusual in the ultrasound to cause me concern."

"Is there anything at all about this pregnancy that is worrying to you?"

"Nothing in the pregnancy. There is only one thing that concerns me."

Antoine becomes very still, his eyes dark and opaque. "Which is?"

Dr. Carter looks at him with her blank eyes. "The father's fear and anger are obvious. In a young couple, such high emotion doesn't bode well, particularly given how hard twins are to manage. It could make the pregnancy harder on the mother. More stressful."

There is a long silence during which Antoine doesn't look at me. Then he sits back in his chair. "Thank you, Dr. Carter," he says, and when her eyes unfocus, he is smiling at her. "You're right," he says, still smiling. "It has been a lot to take in." Reaching over, he takes my hand and meets my eyes for the first time. "But I'm sure that together, we'll manage," he says quietly. "No matter what challenges we face."

Dr. Carter looks between us and nods in satisfaction. "I'm glad to hear that," she says. "Twins are certainly a challenge. The calmer and happier the mother, the greater her chances are of having an easy pregnancy."

"Then I will do everything in my power to ensure she is kept calm and happy."

They continue to talk as I dress. I should feel reassured by Antoine's easy manner, but I don't. I feel a distinct sense of unease.

It's midday as we head out of town. The river glitters in the sun, the sky bright and clear above. The air is potent with the scent of magnolias. They remind me of Tessa, make my heart clench with a fierce sense of urgency. I have to find a way to get back to her.

"Now that we know everything is okay," I say, "we can try to find a way to get me back again, so I can give Tessa the pendants."

"You're not going back, Harper." Antoine's voice is quiet, but very certain. I turn in my seat, and although I can only see his face in profile, what I see makes my heart sink. I've seen that implacable look before. Antoine has made his mind up, and ancient granite is likely to be more pliable than he will be in changing it.

"I know I go back. Tessa told me I do."

"Perhaps you go back after the twins are born. She didn't say that you were pregnant when you visited her, did she?"

I pause, considering that. "No," I say uneasily. "I guess not."

"Then you don't know. If you really do go back, isn't it just as likely that you go after the twins are born—or even when they are grown? You don't know how it works, Harper. It's the twins who travel through time, not you. Shouldn't we wait for them to explain to us how it works?"

"But that could take years." I stare at him. "Years, Antoine. I'm not sure we have that kind of time."

"And I'm not going to risk losing you in an experiment that puts you and the twins at risk." Pulling the car off the road, Antoine turns to me, taking my hands in his. Despite the gentleness of his touch and voice, I can see the steel behind his eyes. "You heard what Dr. Carter said. You need to remain calm. We both do. Stress will make the pregnancy harder on you. Dangerous, even. I won't allow anything to put you in danger."

"Stress?" It takes all my restraint not to roll my eyes. "Antoine, how stressful do you think I'm going to find it spending the next seven months wondering if I ever manage to get back, scared that I don't—that somehow all this will just disappear one day because I didn't?"

"I think that instead of worrying about something we have no control over, we should concern ourselves with what we can control. Right now, you are pregnant and healthy. Let's put all our efforts into ensuring you remain that way, Harper. Okay?" His eyes on mine are dark with emotion, looking right inside me. "The doctor was right," he says, his voice low. "I *am* afraid, Harper. I'm terrified. But not about time travel, or whether we will or won't discover the secrets behind your experience. I'm terrified of losing you." He cups my face, his palm warm and steady against my skin, and I lean into it, unexpected tears tightening my throat. "I can't lose you," Antoine says, his voice rough. "I can't, Harper. I won't. We just need to survive this. Keep you safe from Keziah, healthy, until after the twins are born. Then we can talk about time travel, I promise. We can talk about anything you want. But between now and the birth, I need you to promise me that you'll let this go. Until you're safe, Harper, and no longer carrying the twins inside you, I need to know that you won't try anything that might hurt you."

"I want to promise you that." I cover his hand with my own. "But what if that promise means I am putting *them* at risk, Antoine? How can you ask me to put my own life above the lives of our children?"

"I can ask it because right now, there is no difference between the two." Antoine's hand tenses on my face. "I don't know what mysteries we'll face once they are born, Harper. But I need to know that whatever they are, you'll be alive so we can face them together. Because without you—" His voice breaks off and he looks away, through the windshield, then down at where my other hand is interlaced with his. "Without you," he says quietly, "I don't think I could face any of it."

I want to answer him, give him the reassurance he seeks, but the words are stuck in my chest. I can't utter them. I can't make a promise I know I may not keep.

We sit there for a long time, with only the sounds of the gentle summer breeze and the birds singing in the distance.

Finally, he starts the engine and we drive slowly home, my hand still interlaced with his, my unmade promise a dark shadow hanging in the air between us.

CHAPTER 12

FLOWERS

With every day that passes, my feelings of urgency grow.

I hide them as best I can from Antoine, who is treating me with a solicitude and care that would be the envy of many expecting mothers but instead sets my teeth on edge. I don't want to be cared for. I want to get back to Tessa and make sure my babies are safe.

My impatience isn't helped by the need to conceal what happened from everyone except Callie and Jeremiah.

"Have you found out any more about Iara and the Warao?" I ask them in one of our rare moments alone. Iara is on the porch with Tate, who is teaching her to play chess. The sound of her laughter and, even more unusually, Tate's drifts down the slope to where we're working in the garden.

"Not much." Jeremiah pulls a weed and tosses it aside. "Iara was young when she was taken away from her tribe. She knows a lot about plant medicines and basic healing, but not a great deal about the history of the Warao, or anything at all about the Taíno. I don't think she even understood where Haiti was when I showed her on a map. She's lived a very sheltered life until now. She knew barely anything of the world outside her settlement." We've all been amused at times by Iara's wide-eyed wonder at everything from the local supermarket and drugstore to the intricacies of social media. It doesn't surprise me that she is unaware of the role her own people played in settlement on distant shores. "I'm parched." Jeremiah stands up, stretching his back. "Do either of you want something to drink while I'm there?"

Callie waits until he's wandered uphill before asking in a low voice, "Have you thought any more about going back in time again?"

"It's all I think about." I stab the earth unkindly with my fork. "But Antoine would be furious to know I'm even thinking about it. And I've no more idea how to go back than I did when I went the first time."

"You know you need water and the pendants. And a photo, maybe?"

"Sure." I touch the two pendants, which hang around my neck now. I never take them off, something I know makes Antoine uneasy, though he's never challenged me. I think he knows that on this, I am as immovable as he is on the topic of my time traveling while pregnant. It's a stalemate neither of us has yet found a way to break. "But it's like knowing the ingredients of a recipe without having an explanation of the method. I know what I need to have in order to go, but I don't know how to do it." I don't add that I've stood in the pond more than once and willed myself to disappear. I'm never too certain if I'm relieved or disappointed when nothing happens.

"Iara seems to know a lot about her mother's shamanic practices. Maybe you should ask her." Callie shoots me a wary glance, as if she's thought hard about this and is still unconvinced she's doing the right thing.

"Antoine doesn't want anyone to know."

"I understand that. But honestly—how harmful do you think

Iara actually is?" We turn to look toward the porch, and right on cue, Iara says something that makes both Jeremiah and Tate roar with laughter and bend over Tate's cellphone, clearly showing her something on the internet. It happens a hundred times every day, a mention of something in pop culture that is completely alien to Iara. Our internet service is getting a lot of data usage answering her questions. Callie raises her eyebrows at me with a wry smile. "Seriously," she says. "How dangerous do you really think she is?"

"I don't think she's dangerous at all. But I made a promise to Antoine, and I should at least try to honor it." *Especially since I couldn't give him the promise he really wanted*, I think, but don't say.

As I finish speaking, Iara materializes beside us. I have to force myself not to jump. "I should be used to sudden appearances by now," I say, forcing myself to smile at her, "but somehow it never gets normal, the way you guys just appear like that." I'm speaking in English, at Iara's request. She has picked up the language with a startling rapidity, something Antoine tells me is yet another vampiric gift, though not one all vampires care to exploit. Iara speaks with a noticeable accent, and still struggles with certain phrases, but to me, her pace of learning is nothing less than astonishing.

"I am sorry." Iara's face falls, her faltering English soft and unsteady. "I did not mean to scare."

"It's fine, really." I touch her arm to show there are no hard feelings and turn back to my gardening.

"You have many special plants here." Iara touches the tightly furled water lilies that are just showing above the water. "These come when you are pregnant, *si?*"

"Yes," I say, looking at her in surprise. "How did you know?"

She shrugs. "Is normal. Your garden, your babies. You must take care of these flowers." She holds her hand just over the burgeoning stalks and closes her eyes, as if she's feeling them.

"Strong," she murmurs. "Roots deep in water. Is good." Then a moment later, she becomes very still. Her eyes fly open and lock on my belly.

"What is it?" I say, unable to keep the fear from my voice. "What is it that you can see?"

"They are scared," Iara says. "There is a reason flowers are not blooming. What is it, Harper? Why do they not come to life?"

I want to keep my promise to Antoine. But Iara's face is so concerned, her eyes so soft and understanding, that I feel my resolve weaken. I glance at Callie, who nods. "Tell her," Callie urges. "What can it hurt, Harper? She might be able to help."

In halting sentences, with Callie's help, I give Iara a brief overview of the situation. I keep waiting for her to recoil in shock or disbelief, but she listens gravely, asking the odd question here or there, but overall seems so unsurprised that it is almost disconcerting.

"You seem very calm," I say, as I come to the end of my story. Iara tilts her head to one side.

"With my people," she says, "such things are not so strange. Here, time is something you count on a line. You have these clocks everywhere. On your telephones, your wall, your wrist. Everything is organized by these numbers, this counting. It never stops. It is maybe the most strange thing for me to learn—that it is this day, or that. This time, or another. With us it is not like this."

"But you have time, surely? Even if you count it differently. By the moon, for example, or seasons." It's such a strange concept, to imagine a world where time lacks the significance it does here.

"Yes, we have change, is true, the movement of the earth. But not time. Not so it is past, or present, or future. These are not words we speak of so much in my language." She shakes her head. "Is hard to explain. Some of my people understand secrets of moving between the worlds, of walking the water paths that lead from one experience to another."

"Between time, you mean? Your people can travel through time?" I stare at her. "Can you help me to do the same?"

"We do not call it this *travel through time*, like you say. For us is water paths."

"Water paths, then. Can you teach me how to walk them?"

"I do not know these secrets." She looks at me doubtfully. "But maybe I can help you to be in right place, inside and outside, so maybe the water paths take you." She leans forward and pulls the chains up so she can see the pendants. Her eyes seem to glow briefly, but I realize it must be the light reflecting off the pendants. "You have some tools already," she says.

"But that's what I don't understand." I put the pendants back under my shirt, uneasy with anyone other than myself touching them. "If I take these pendants back in time and leave them there, then how can I be sure I am safe myself on the return journey? How will I do it?"

"This is easy enough. You say they hold blood from you and Antoine?"

I nod. "I think so, yes."

Iara shrugs. "So you do not need pretty necklace. You take a little of Antoine's blood, a little of yours. We mix with river water, also. Put in a jar. Is a good moon for this tonight. We can do together, if you like. So long as you carry with you is same as jewelry."

"Do you really think so?" I look at Callie and see she is as excited as I am. "And you really believe you can help me?"

Iara puts her hand over mine, her eyes liquid chocolate, sad and soft at once. "You have given me home," she says quietly. "Family." She colors faintly. "Tate." Seeing the way Iara glances up the slope, I realize that perhaps it is more than just loyalty to an old friend that has bound Tate so firmly to her side. "Please," she says, squeezing my hand. "After all you do for me, perhaps this is one thing I can do for you."

I look at Callie, who nods. "I honestly think you have to try," she says quietly. "Even though I know Antoine will hate it."

"Then we won't tell him." When Callie opens her mouth to protest, I glare at her until she shuts it again. "He will never allow it, Callie," I say, hearing the pleading in my voice. "If we do this, it has to be a secret. Antoine is too scared of what might happen to me if I try."

"And you're not?"

"I'm terrified." I hold her eyes. "But I'm even more terrified that if I don't, my twins will never make it into this world. I have to go back. If I don't, I may end up—" I'm about to say, *trapped in another time*, but then I remember what Iara said. "Trapped on another water path. Perhaps I never return to this time from that one, or even worse, perhaps my babies are never born at all. And what happens if I don't go back, and the pendants are never planted—will they simply disappear? I can't risk that, Callie. This is my home. My life. I don't want to lose it. And I need to know my babies can find their way back to me, no matter where they might find themselves."

I turn to Iara. "How do we do this?"

"I will tell you." We lean in close, and as Jeremiah and Tate laugh on the porch behind us, Iara explains what we are going to do.

CHAPTER 13

BATON ROUGE

Despite my eagerness, it's nonetheless an entire week before the perfect opportunity to return to Tessa arises. Unfortunately, I'm going to have to contend with Antoine's presence as well.

"I thought you might like to come to Baton Rouge with us." I know Antoine means it as a peace offering. "A friend of Tate's who knew Ramon well is going to be in Baton Rouge a little while. Tate can't go because he's teaching, so I offered to take Iara to Baton Rouge to meet him and see if he might know more about why Ramon went to South America. I thought you could visit your mom's grave. If you wanted to."

"I'd love to." I don't dare look at Iara. She told me our plan has a higher chance of success if I use the same fountain outside the Baton Rouge hospital in which I arrived last time. "Is less complicated," she explained. "Less chance for wrong path."

I'm all for less chances.

I managed to get some of Antoine's blood, too, another obstacle I had thought would be harder than it turned out to be. All it took was a casual mention that I understood our mingled blood served as an anchor to this time and place for Antoine to return with a vial and strict instructions for me to carry it, always. It hurt me to deceive him, but not as much as it hurt to imagine my life without him, or the twins, in it. I mixed my blood with his under the light of the moon, according to Iara's instructions. I did it alone. Antoine's suspicions would never allow me to remain alone with Iara. Besides, there was something so potent in the blending of our blood that I was glad, once I started, that I was alone. It seemed like I could feel the magic in the mixture, thick and heavy, and when I added river water, the liquid seemed to gleam with a dark, heady power that made me shiver.

Since then, I've found that wearing the vial close to my skin gives me a warm feeling of comfort. The vial seems to almost throb with power. It feels connected to the two pendants, but different, also. Though I can't help but wonder if that is just my own fancy.

On the day we are to drive to Baton Rouge, I put everything I will need inside a backpack: the photo of Tessa from my bedside, the jar of potion from the garden, a lily from the pond. Avery arrives at the mansion with Callie, Cass, and Jeremiah, and I go out onto the porch to greet them It's almost as hard to look them in the eye as it is Antoine. Only Callie knows my plans, and with her customary discretion, she stays in the background.

"Are you sure you don't want company?" Avery asks. "I remember how emotional you were last time you visited your mom's grave." She's making a real effort to reestablish our friendship.

"No." I smile at her gratefully. "I think it's better if I go alone this time. I have some things I need to say aloud." *But not to Mom*, I think guiltily. It's Tessa I'm hoping to speak to by the end of today, though I know it won't be easy to pull off. "What are you guys doing here, anyway?" I ask as Avery walks by me into the house, casting a disdainful glance at Callie as she goes.

"We plan to spend the day sleuthing." Cass smiles at me. Despite the wary shadow behind her eyes, I know she, too, is trying hard to be friends. I can't imagine how difficult it must be for her, knowing I am pregnant—and that she will never be. "Jeremiah thinks my vamp speed might be put to good use going through the academic papers he's collected on the Warao. We're seeing what we can discover about Ramon's background, anything that might help discover why Ramon was down there in the first place."

"It can't be coincidence," Jeremiah says. "He clearly knew something we didn't. We need to find out if maybe that something can help defeat Keziah."

"Tate's going to call ahead to the friend you're visiting, ask a few questions," Cass adds. "And we might call again while you're there, so leave your phones on."

"Here." Avery holds out my backpack, smiling. "I put a sweater inside for you. It's cool out." I try not to snatch the backpack from her, unable to stop myself casting her a sideways glance, wondering what she saw when she opened the pack. But Avery is talking to Cass, with no hint of suspicion in her face. I breathe a sigh of relief. The last thing I need is Avery's sharp tongue making a tactless comment.

Antoine is driving the sleek, black Mercedes that spends most of its life in the shed at the river house. "More comfortable for long distance than the truck," he grins at me when I comment on the change. "And besides," he murmurs in too low a tone to be heard by the others, "I couldn't drive all the way to Baton Rouge with you on the bench seat next to me. We wouldn't make it past the first motel."

Since even the thought of that makes my heart thud in a way that has nothing to do with time travel, I get into the car trying my hardest not to touch him as he holds the door. "Our wedding day," he says as I pass him. "That's the last time we were in this car together."

Since those memories are even more potent than the previous images, I put my head down and try to focus on what is coming. Iara, in the seat behind me, is white-faced and tense, and I'm touched that she seems almost as nervous as I am.

We drive in silence down the highway. I don't trust myself to speak. Iara has discovered the joys of headphones and is happily plugged in to some music Tate has loaded for her. Antoine is staring straight ahead, shooting me smiles he no doubt intends to be reassuring. I can see the tension behind them, however, and if I speak, he will sense mine. I turn to look out the window and feign exhaustion. It isn't difficult; lately I could sleep twenty hours of the day, given the choice.

We are nearing a turnoff to a gas station when Antoine's phone beeps with a text message. He pulls it out while still driving, and I stifle a smile. Vampires, I've learned as time goes by, simply don't follow the rules. Then I see the suddenly grim expression on his face, the way he glances sharply in the rearview mirror, and fear grips my belly.

"I'll stop so you can use the bathroom, Harper," he says, loudly enough to penetrate Iara's headphones. She looks up, and Antoine smiles at her in the mirror. "We won't be long," he says. "But you should probably stay in the car, Iara. It's better if people don't see your face so much. You never know who is watching."

The car is barely at a halt when he is out of it and opening my door. "Walk toward the bathroom as if nothing is wrong," he breathes in my ear, pressing my backpack into my hand and turning away so Iara can't see his face. "Tate just sent a message. There's a chance Iara is under Keziah's control."

"Iara?" Startled, I face him. "But she can't be." Even as I say it, in my peripheral vision I see Iara reaching for her door. Her eyes gleam with a sharp red light. "She knows," I say, fear clenching my chest.

"You need to go, Harper. Keziah could be anywhere close

by." Antoine is pushing me toward the bathroom, opening the door and urging me inside.

"Go where?" I can see Iara moving out of the car, teeth bared, eyes flashing red.

"I know you were planning to travel." For a brief moment Antoine's eyes hold mine, and I see my own fear mirrored in his. "If you know how to do it, Harper, then go. Now. I can't keep you safe. Not if there are two of them."

My own fear is something I have come to live with. Seeing Antoine's, however, is different. The desperation in his eyes sends cold terror through my veins. He whirls away to face Iara, and I clutch the sink behind me, frozen in place as the two vampires meet in a savage, snarling whirl of limbs and teeth. My hand closes around the pendants on my neck so the filigree silver cuts into my fingers, my other hand clutching the strap of the backpack. I back further into the small space, pressing up against the sink until the tap spurts into life behind me, running over the base of my spine. Iara is fighting to get past Antoine, her eyes intent on me. This is not the soft, gentle Iara I know, but a raging fury, intent on murder.

I've seen that rage before. In Keziah's face.

In my side vision, I see a flicker of color, just a hint of movement but enough to trigger my internal alarm. What if Keziah is already here?

Fear seizes me, and I close my eyes. "Take me to Tessa," I whisper, feeling the water behind me and the heat of the pendants in my hand, the weight of my pack on my shoulder. I put my other hand on my belly, searching for the lives within. "Please, if you can hear me, take me to Tessa. Now."

The world slips, and darkness takes me. I tumble through the pathways. It seems quicker this time, as if there is clearer direction to my journey. I feel something hard pressing against my back. I realize it is a sink, and for a moment, I fear I am still in the bathroom at the gas station, and I have gone nowhere.

Then I open my eyes to clinical white and blue. The sink behind me is the one in the corner of Tessa's hospital room. My sister is sitting up in bed, sheet clutched to her throat, staring at me in wide-eyed shock.

"Harper," she whispers. "Where did you come from?"

CHAPTER 14

GOODBYE

"*Tessa*." I stay where I am, watching my twin warily, conscious of her stunned expression and all too familiar with what she is feeling. "I know this must seem impossible."

"You're older." Tessa is still staring at me, but her initial shock has given way to an almost feverish excitement. Her eyes travel down to my hand, then to my belly. "You're wearing the emerald," she breathes. "It's just like they told me." She looks at me in fascination. "You're pregnant, aren't you?"

Utterly confused, I nod. Tessa shakes her head in wonder. "They told me it would happen. I don't think I believed it. Not until now. I still don't know if I believe it."

"Who told you?" I approach the bed cautiously, worried I will scare her. "How do you know about the emerald?"

"The Marigny emerald." Tessa reaches out to take my hand and I feel a faint, bittersweet shock at her touch. "That means you did meet him. Antoine. Are you married yet? Oh," she says, as if catching herself in a mistake. "Of course you are. But you haven't had your proper wedding. Not yet. But you are pregnant." She looks at the pendants on my neck. "It's just like they said," she says, in that same wondering tone.

Even through my shock, her eyes on the pendants jolt me into remembering what I am here to do. I reach up to unclasp them from around my neck. "Before I tell you what is happening," I say, "I have to ask you to put these somewhere safe. Tomorrow I will come here again, and when I do, I need you to give me these things." I put the backpack on the bed and pull out the jar of liquid. The photo of Tessa falls out with it. She picks it up and stares at it.

"It hasn't been taken yet," I say. "I know it doesn't make any sense, Tessa. But later today I'm going to come and visit you— not me, exactly, but a different version of me." I stop, unsure how to go on.

"It's okay, Harper." Tessa takes my hand again. She is looking at me with the same fascination she has since I appeared in the corner of her room. "I know this is a future version of you. They told me you would come. They warned me. I guess a part of me just didn't believe it. Not until right now, with you standing here." She picks up the photograph. "This is from today?"

I nod, though I'm so confused that when I answer, my words are disjointed. "Yes, the photo is from today, and I need to make sure it's taken, Tessa, and that I—the old me—puts it in a frame and keeps it. You need to make me understand it's important to you." I stop, unsure what I am even saying. "Tessa." I stare at her. "The last time I was here, you said the twins told you I would come. I didn't have time to ask you any more about it. But now I have to know. You said you met my twins, Tessa." I can barely get the words out.

"Yes." Tessa covers my hand with both of hers, her clear emerald eyes warm and reassuring on mine. "I can't tell you their names—it's one of the rules. But I've met your twins,

Harper. Many times. They've been coming to visit me ever since we were very young."

"Then that means they live. We survive this." My throat closes over, the familiar tears threatening again.

"Of course you survive this. Your twins are beautiful, Harper. They are going to bring you so much joy." The longing in her voice brings a jagged sound from my throat, half laugh, half sob.

"Here we are," I say unevenly, "me, time traveling, and you—"

"Dying," she finishes dryly. Once, long ago, when I'd sat by her bedside, I couldn't bear it when she made these jokes, had become angry and upset. But now, with the years between her death and the miracle of seeing her again, I, too, can smile.

"Dying," I say softly. I squeeze her hand. "And yet still you find a way to say the one thing I need to hear more than anything else." The same tears catching my throat glisten in Tessa's eyes, turning them to the brilliant aqua of a high mountain lake.

"It's my final gift to you, Harper," she says. "And we have time today. We have hours before you come to visit. Time for me to tell you everything you need to know."

"Can you tell me about them?" I touch my belly. "About my twins?"

"A little, yes." She smiles sadly. "But there are rules, Harper, like I said. I will tell you what I can."

"When did you first know about them?"

"Do you remember the day we were playing hide-and-seek in the garden, in our old house by the river, when we were little? It was before Gareth, Connor's dad, came to live with us. We had a fight, because I told you I'd been playing with two friends, and you said there was nobody else there."

"I remember!" I can almost feel the bark on the old oak, smell the river thick and slow, the red magnolia petals on the ground around me. "It was summer," I say slowly. "I was hiding, waiting for you to seek me out, and you didn't come. I hid for so long I fell asleep. When I woke up, hours had passed. You were crying. You said you'd made some new friends, but you wouldn't tell me about them, and when I wanted to meet them, you said I couldn't. I was cross with you for days."

"That was the first time they came to me." Tessa smiles. "I can barely remember it now, or not much of it. They were very young, maybe seven or eight. Certainly not too old to play with me. They kept giggling and whispering to one another. They made me promise not to tell you they'd met me—they said you'd be mad. I didn't understand why. I just thought they were fascinating. Then they stepped into the river, and suddenly they were gone. I cried for days."

"But you saw them again?"

Tessa nods. "I was ten the next time they came. They were older, though, and I didn't recognize them at first. They were about the age we are now—sixteen. They came to the hospital the first time I got sick. They stayed all night, playing games with me, reading to me . . ." her voice breaks off, and she looks away for a moment, collecting herself. "I think they were the only ones who really understood how lonely and scared I was. Nobody knew then, how sick I was, but I did. Inside me, I knew. And I hated that everyone kept telling me I'd be fine, when I knew I wasn't fine at all. They understood that." She smiles at me. "After that, they came all the time. Whenever I was alone, or needed someone to talk to, they would come. They've been with me through all the surgeries. Whenever I woke up in the middle of the night, alone in hospital. Sometimes it seems all I have to do is think of them, and they come. It was only when I got a little older that I wondered why, since they were older than me, that they always called me Auntie Tessa."

"How old?" I can barely get the words out. It's so much to try to comprehend. "How old are they now, Tessa?"

"I've never seen them older than their early twenties." Fear, swift and dark, clutches at my belly. I try to keep it from my eyes as Tessa continues. "They come at different ages, even now. Sometimes they are barely teenagers, other times they are in their early twenties. But they told me to tell you not to worry about that." She smiles at me with understanding, and I know she has seen my fear. "There is a good reason for it, one you will understand in time."

"It's so hard for me to understand." I stroke her hand, trying to make sense of it. "Then we are all . . . okay?" I pause, ashamed of my own self-interest, but also unable to contain my questions. "Antoine? Did they tell you that he—what he is?"

"They told me that he is extraordinary, Harper. They love him so much. They love you both." She searches my face. "I don't need to know what he is," she says quietly. "I know there are things about your world now that belong to magic, things that I couldn't begin to understand. I used to want to know it all. Sometimes I even got mad they wouldn't tell me. But now that I'm close to the end . . ." She shrugs, giving me a lopsided smile. "Now, it all seems like a miracle. I just want you to know that I love you, Harper. I love you all. And I need you to tell Connor something."

"Of course." I'm trying so hard to hold myself together, when all I want to do is break down.

"Tell him that having him as my brother was the greatest gift I was ever given. That I will love him forever. And that I will always, always be there, if he needs to talk."

"He needs to know that," I whisper. "We both do. Tessa, there are times I hear you—in the wind, in the flowers. Sometimes it feels like you are so close I could touch you."

"I *am* there, Harper." She grips my hand with an odd strength. "This is the thing I am allowed to tell you. I *am* there. Not in the way you see me now, but I am there nonetheless. There are pathways in trees and flowers, Harper. On the wind.

You feel me in the red magnolia trees. Connor—he has his own plant, the place he goes to feel safe. Tell him I am there. It isn't his imagination. It isn't yours. When you feel that breeze on your face, hear me on the wind, or in the water—it is real, Harper. I am there. I will always be there. I promise. And particularly in your night garden, Harper. Where you put my ashes." She squeezes my hand. "Don't let anyone else tell you what to do with them after I die. You take them, and put me in your garden, Harper, so I can help you and your family. Promise me."

I try to smile. "I promise."

"Good. And now there is something else." Tessa nods at the bedside dresser. "Open the drawer. Inside it you'll find a stone figurine."

I do. The drawer has something scented inside it, and the smell makes my head swirl with memories. I recall it from Tessa's last days, an oddly wild scent. It reminds me of the bayous.

I find what I'm looking for and lift it out. The figurine depicts a woman, squatting frog-like, her mouth open. It is small, at once beautiful and menacing, the carved lines smooth with age. "Take it back with you," she says. "Give it to Iara. It will break her compulsion, free her from Keziah's control."

"I can't have Iara anywhere near me," I say, shuddering with the recollection of her face, furious and intent, as I backed into the bathroom. "She's dangerous."

"She won't be after you give her this. And she will help you, one day. With Keziah. This is important, Harper, do you understand?"

"Sure, I understand." I laugh shakily. "Even years after I lost you, you're still bossy, Tessa."

She laughs softly. "Indulge me. It's the last time I get to boss you around."

"It can't be the last time." I study her face, my heart tightening as her smile fades. "Can't I keep visiting you? Now that I know how?"

Tessa shakes her head slowly. "It's the twins who can travel, Harper, not you."

"But they could bring me back, after they're born—"

"No." Her voice is definite. "Even if they could, you can't travel back to a time before their birth."

"And their birth is after . . ." I speak without thinking and bite my lip when I realize what I'm saying.

"After I die yes." Tessa draws an uneven breath. I grasp her hands.

"I'm so sorry." My tears are unstoppable now, spilling down my face to fall on the coverlet between us. "If I could have stopped it, I would have, Tessa. If there was anything—*anything* —I could have done, I would have done it. I still can. Is there anything?" But I know, even as I'm saying the words, that there isn't. Something in me knows I can't stop what is coming.

"There isn't anything." Tears shine on her cheeks, but they aren't tears of grief; they are some deeper emotion, some mixture of love and resignation that feels far more potent. I know grief well. I've lived with its dull edges for what seems like forever. What I see in Tessa's face is something much more beautiful. "I'm ready to go," she whispers, turning my hand over in hers.

"You tried to tell me that." I remember, suddenly, this exact look in her eyes. "You tried so hard to tell me you were ready to go. But I couldn't hear it."

"No, you certainly don't want to hear it. Or the old you, the you I know, doesn't. Connor, either." She laughs shakily. "Sometimes it's—exhausting. I want you to know I'm ready to go. It's like I can't let go, so long as you don't know that. It's like an anchor holding me to this life. And I'm so tired, Harper. I'm so tired of waking up every day."

"Then will you hear me now?" I drop her hands and cradle her face. I know, suddenly, that this is the thing I can do, the only gift still in my power to give my sister. "In the years after you go," I say softly, "I regretted a thousand times that I couldn't say goodbye to you. Not even at the very end, when I knew you were taking your last breaths. I didn't know how to let you go then—and afterward, I hated myself for that, for not giving you peace. I couldn't even talk to Connor about it. The guilt crippled me. Him, too. I know he wishes he could have done it differently, even if he can't admit it. So let me do it now, Tessa. For Connor and me."

I stroke the hair back from her face, and for the first time, I see my sister's composure crack, the fear and loneliness come into her eyes. "I'm so scared, Harper," she whispers, her voice breaking on the words. "I'm so scared it will hurt, that I won't be brave."

"You listen to me, Tessa." My thumbs brush the tears from under her eyes. "You are the bravest person I know. In your last days, Connor and I never leave you. One of us holds your hand the entire time. You just slip into darkness, into peace, and finally, you simply stop breathing. It is a quiet passing, a peaceful one. The pain is gone. You just let go. And I need you to know this, Tessa, so listen to me carefully: no matter what the old me says to you in the next few days, or what Connor says, we understand that you have to go. I *want* you to go. I want this to be over for you, and I want you to know, too, that Connor and I—we never, ever forget you. I will never let my babies forget you." She sobs, and I wrap my arms around her, feeling her frail body shake against me as she cries. "I will tell them to visit their Auntie Tessa," I whisper. "I will remember all the times you were sick, or alone, and I will tell them to go to you, and to be there for you, and that way, even though I don't have you, they will. I swear they will know you and love you through it all. I will never abandon you."

"And I will never leave you," she whispers against my shoulder. "I promise you, Harper. I will always be there."

I hold her close as my sister cries on my shoulder, and it is the most peace I have known since the day she died.

CHAPTER 15

HOME

$\mathcal{A}$ long time later, Tessa pulls away, wiping her eyes. She points to the jar with the mixture in it. "What is that?"

"Something I made to help me get back." I explain the potion I mixed from the garden to her.

"Does it actually work?" She eyes it skeptically.

"I'm not sure." I shrug. "It seemed like it did, somehow."

"When?"

"When I come to see you tomorrow." Hastily I explain the visit the following day. "But I will have no time," I say, "and I won't understand anything that is going on. So this has to be our goodbye. Tomorrow we have no time for this, for any of it, but I know now that today we do—we have this visit, uninterrupted. So tomorrow there are only a few things I need to know." I try to remember the important points. "The most important thing is these pendants," I say, pointing to them. "You told me that I have to take them with me, that I must keep them on me at all times." I frown. "But I still don't understand how you have them. You said I gave them to you, but I don't know how. I didn't make them. I even had to make a backup so that I can get back."

Tessa laughs softly. "The pendants are made especially for the twins, but they don't know exactly how. They have them from infancy," she says. "They said you'd work it out and make something for yourself."

I shake my head. "I'm starting to get an irresistible urge to apply some discipline to these twins of mine."

Tessa gives such a loud gurgle of laughter that I find myself openly laughing, too. "Oh," she says, wagging her finger at me, "believe me, you do. The first time they come to visit me they get in so much trouble when they go back that they don't dare travel for years afterward. A hint?" She winks at me. "They're wearing matching fairy costumes. Watch out for that."

"Noted," I say, but it's so good to see her smiling, see the color in her face, that I'm barely listening.

She reaches into the dresser and hands me a daisy. "This comes from the gas station where Iara attacked you. The twins got it for me—they said you almost saw them."

I remember the odd flicker in my side vision. "I did," I say wonderingly. "I thought I saw someone—then they were gone." I frown. "Wait—does that mean the twins have been here today, with you?"

Tessa's mouth curves into a secret smile. "They are here every moment that you are not," she says quietly. "They are here when I wake, and when I sleep. They are my greatest comfort."

"They are the friends the nurses kept telling us about!" I have a sudden realization. "The two girls with beautiful hair. Connor and I never knew who they were talking about—we thought they had you confused with another patient." I look around, a strange hope stealing over me.

"You can't see them." Tessa answers my unspoken question. "Technically, you're not supposed to even know they are girls."

"Twin girls," I breathe. "Just like us."

She nods sadly. "Just like us. But so special, Harper. So incredibly special." She grips my hand and puts the daisy in it.

"Now you should go," she says firmly. "And as soon as you get back, hand Iara the stone figurine. Apparently it will break her compulsion, and you will be safe. And you have to convince Antoine she isn't a threat. No matter how much he argues." Her mouth twitches. "Is it wrong of me to like the fact that you have someone so strong in your life? He must be amazing, Harper, if you love him."

"Why?" I look at her, puzzled.

"Because your heart is secret, Harper. It always has been. You don't let anyone see it—and you don't let anyone love it. If you've let him see you, the real you, he must be special indeed."

"He is." I shake my head. "I wish you knew him, Tessa. I wish he knew you."

She smiles, and leans in close. "You never know," she whispers in my ear. "You never know, Harper."

There are footsteps in the corridor, and she lets go of my hands. "You have to go now," she says. "That's the doctor on her rounds."

"Goodbye, Tessa," I hold her eyes, trying to keep my voice steady. I owe her this one last, smiling goodbye, free of tears or false reassurances.

"Goodbye for you, maybe." She smiles at me. "But I will see you tomorrow, Harper."

"Sure." I turn the tap on in the sink, holding my sister's eyes. "I'll see you tomorrow." I'm still smiling at her when the room fades, and I tumble into darkness.

~

I OPEN MY EYES TO DAZZLING SUNLIGHT. I'M STANDING IN A TUB of water against the back wall of the gas station. Daisies like the one I hold grow around the base of the tub. I hear the savage sounds of Antoine and Iara fighting around the corner. Stepping gingerly out of the tub, I edge to the corner and peer around.

Iara has her back to me, but Antoine's eyes widen in shock when he sees me. I know why. Barely a second ago, he closed the door to the bathroom behind me, and now I'm coming from a different direction, holding a stone figure he hasn't seen before. *Trust me.* I mouth the words as I walk slowly toward the struggling figures, ignoring the fury in Antoine's.

"Iara," I say quietly.

She spins around, snarling, and crouches, ready to pounce. I hold up the stone figurine. "This is for you. You need it, Iara." She lunges toward me, making a guttural sound of savage delight that chills me to the bone. I force myself to stand my ground, thrusting the stone figure into her hands as they reach for me. I close my eyes, bracing myself for impact, then, when it doesn't come, crack one warily open.

Iara is standing still, staring down at the figurine, her mouth a perfect O of surprise. Slowly she raises her eyes to me, and I see they are clear, all trace of red savagery gone, the soft chocolate of the gentle girl I know once more. "Harper?" she says uncertainly. "How did I get here?"

"It's okay, Iara," I say, gently, coming toward her with my hand outstretched. "You're going to be fine. You were compelled."

Antoine is at my side, pulling me close to him. "It's okay." I touch his cheek. "She won't hurt me now."

"We need to get her away from you." Antoine's face is dark with rage. "She was going to kill you, Harper."

"No." I hold his eyes. "You have to listen to me, Antoine: Iara won't hurt me. She's going to help us with Keziah. I promise you, she is important. We need her."

"How do you know that?" He frowns, scrutinizing my face. "And how did you get out of the bathroom? Is there a window?"

"I traveled," I say softly. "I went back, Antoine. I saw Tessa."
My eyes fill with tears. "I saw her for the last time."

"You went?" Fear and wonder chase across his eyes, and his
hands come up to hold my face, Iara forgotten. "Tell me you're
okay, Harper. Tell me our babies are okay—"

"They're fine." I smile tremulously. "They're better than fine,
Antoine. They're amazing."

"You saw them?"

"I didn't see them. But Tessa has. They've been visiting her.
Or they will visit her." I shake my head. "It's hard to explain."

"Harper." I turn to Iara, and Antoine pulls me closer to his
side, all trace of amiability gone from his face. "I am sorry," Iara
whispers. "I do not remember—just a woman, her face. The
same one who killed Ramon."

"Keziah." I nod. "She was controlling you, Iara. But you're
okay now. She can't hurt you anymore."

"But what if I hurt you?" Iara is backing away, her eyes wide
with fear and pain. "What if I hurt you without knowing?"

"You won't." I nod at the figurine. "Do you know what
that is?"

She looks down at it and nods, slowly. "It is from temple in
my village. A carving of the Abatey. It helps with my mother's
healing. For women in my family, it can break any bind others
might put on us."

"Does that mean you are no longer controlled by Keziah?"
Antoine is watching her warily. She nods.

"My mind is clear now." She looks at me. "But I don't understand why this Keziah can control me, if she is not my Maker."

"That's just it." Antoine's eyes return to me. "We might have
been mistaken, Iara. It looks like Keziah may have been your
Maker, after all."

CHAPTER 16

MAKER

"It was Jeremiah who first worked it out."

We're sitting on the back porch. Everyone is at the mansion, even Avery, Connor, and Cass. I can't quite look at my brother. I have so much to tell him and no idea where to start. For the moment, at least, I don't need to think about it; all eyes are trained on Tate, listening to him tell us Iara's story.

"Jeremiah called me out of class to ask me who Ramon's Maker was," Tate goes on. "I didn't know, but I knew someone who might: Paolo, the friend of Ramon's you were supposed to visit today. Paolo knew Ramon even longer than I did. They didn't see much of one another in the time I knew him, but I knew they had spent a great deal of time together in earlier days. In fact, I had assumed, I suppose, that Paolo was Ramon's Maker. I emailed him at the address he used to contact me after he heard of Ramon's death. He called me as soon as he got the message and told me that it wasn't him, but Keziah, who was Ramon's Maker."

"Keziah made Ramon?" Antoine's blank shock mirrors my own. "How did we not know this?"

"Believe it or not," Tate says, "we never discussed our

97

Makers. When I met Ramon, you and I had not spoken for almost a century, Antoine, and Ramon had been a vampire for many centuries before that. Ramon and I discussed history and culture, the origin of our species—but never our own Makers." Glancing at me, he shrugs. "Among our kind, such discussions are considered almost sacred. Certainly not topics for idle conversation. Our bonds are intense and timeless. To share them is to share the most intimate corners of our souls. We rarely speak of such matters, even to those closest to us."

I turn to Jeremiah. "What made you think of asking about Ramon's Maker?"

"It was basic deduction. There were too many coincidences. The link between the Warao and the Taíno people. Ramon making a new vampire, when he had explicitly told Tate he didn't believe in making more of his own kind. Then Keziah showing up and killing Ramon, but sparing Iara. There were just too many connections. It made me wonder what links might exist between Ramon and Keziah."

"Keziah had been locked away by the curse in Antoine's cellar for a century when I met Ramon," says Tate. "It was a painful topic for me, and I'm sure he had long considered her gone, or at least safely contained. I never discussed where I came from, and he never asked. It was only recently, after I got in touch, asking if he might know anything about the Taíno or that could help us combat Keziah, that he said he needed to see me. He never said why, only that it was important. I thought he might have discovered something we could use. And then today, when I spoke to Paolo and told him of Ramon's death, he said he had a package Ramon had sent him. He opened it while we were talking and read me the letter inside."

"Can you tell us what was in it?" Antoine asks.

"Better." Tate holds up his phone. "I recorded Paolo reading it." He puts the phone on the table and presses the play icon. A tinny voice with a faint Spanish accent comes through the speaker.

My friend, Paolo—

If you are reading this, then I am certainly finished. This is not sad. I have been too many years on this earth already, so we will not talk more on my death. Instead, I must tell you what I know, while I still can.

I have been compelled by my Maker and cannot confide in my friend, Takatoka, or Tate, as you may know him. So instead I write this letter to you, Paolo, and trust it will find you in time for you to relay it to those who must know the story.

I had thought rumors of Keziah's escape no more than that: rumors. Until I spoke to Tate, and realized that his Maker was Antoine Marigny, and his home the old grounds of the Natchez. Then I knew I must come to warn him of how dangerous she is. Unfortunately, Keziah found me before I could do so.

I have known Keziah for five centuries, but I have never known her as scared as she was then, in the days following Caleb's death. It gave me hope. For the first time, I allowed myself to believe that defeating her might be possible after all. I had long given up hope of ever finding a way to end her existence. I knew very little of her origins other than that she was from the Caribbean; Tate's call was the first time I heard of her connection to the Taíno.

Despite the hope his call brought me, I was as helpless to her compulsion as I have ever been. My bind to Keziah stems from the love I bore her before she turned me. Love, as we all know, is the strongest bind of all. It is not something I have ever found the strength to resist.

She ordered me to make a new vampire. It must be a female, she told me, and young; specifically, seventeen to eighteen years of age. She did not say why, but I am sure she cannot mean anything good by doing such a thing. Keziah does nothing unless it serves her own dark purposes.

But there was something more. Keziah gave me a syringe of her own blood and commanded me to use it to make the newborn. The newborn must believe me to be her Maker, but in reality, she would belong to Keziah.

I hated everything about doing her will, but I was also helpless to defy her, bound to her as I am. She had thought of everything; I could speak of the ruse to no one, find no way out of doing what she asked. But I did think of something which might change whatever evil outcome Keziah wished for. I thought if I could somehow find someone from the Warao people, a powerful shaman, that I could create a weapon to rival Keziah herself. The Warao are older than the Taíno. Their magic is drawn from the Orinoco basin, derived from a time and place predating the Haitian tribe. It is more ancient, more powerful.

Iara's name is one used by many indigenous tribes in South America, to mean "water nymph," or, in some languages, "lady of the water." She is the child of two of the most powerful shamans in her tribe—and I ensured that her first kill was another, also powerful, shaman. Iara has been made using the blood of the most powerful vampire to walk our world, but she is also made of the blood of those who predate Keziah herself.

Keziah is her Maker. Although it was I who drained her, when Iara thought I fed her my blood, it was in fact Keziah's she drank.

I made Iara as a weapon. I paid another shaman from her tribe to bind the sun inside her. I saw it done once before, in Spain, when I fought there long ago. I wanted to give Iara every advantage over Keziah, who must always rely on her talisman to walk in the sun. Keziah, however, knows nothing of Iara's origins and believes Iara to be her tool. She intends to use Iara to defeat her enemies. I am to place Iara inside Tate's family. Keziah will use her to destroy them all, unless Tate can find a way to destroy her first. I do not have time to discover the means by which he might use Iara, or how she might use her powers against Keziah. This, I must entrust to my old friend Tate. And if you are reading Tate the contents of this letter, please tell him it is a task I must sadly leave him to work out alone. I pray he has Antoine, the brother of his heart, to help. I wish I had known the truth of his connection to Antoine Marigny. I must hope, too, that their rift is mended. Our lives are long. But I trust that this letter is evidence that they also end, often violently and abruptly. I do not wish for any of my friends to waste what time they have.

Let Tate not fear that he cannot win against Keziah. I believe that if anyone can, it is he.

I have compelled Iara to find him, even if I am not with her. Tell Tate to care for her. She may not be mine by blood, but she is my child—and I entrust her to him.

Be strong, my friends.

Ramon.

In the silence that follows, we turn one by one to look at Iara. She, however, looks only at Tate. "I belong to Keziah," she says flatly. "Ramon was never my Maker."

"Yes." Tate's hand closes over hers. "But you heard him. He loved you, Iara. As do we. You are safe with us." He holds her eyes, and I can sense the battle inside her. Finally, her rigid form relaxes, and with a small sigh, she leans against Tate. He puts his arm around her and holds her close, looking at Antoine over her head. "I won't let you send her away."

Antoine's mouth twitches. "I see that," he says gently. "Iara." He leans forward and smiles kindly. "Can you tell me about Keziah? Can you—feel her, inside you?"

"*Si.*" Iara nods. "I hear her, also. But now, since I have the statue, is like I hear her—I feel her—but from far away. I know she is there, but she does not command me. I feel nothing, like watching your television."

"Is she calling you now?"

"*Si.* Ever since the time in the gas station, she talks to me, asking me to come, come. To bring this one." Iara nods at me, then her face crumples. "I am so sorry I hurt you," she whispers, tears sliding down her face. "I would never hurt you—the babies—"

"I know, Iara." I grasp her hand. "Truly, I do. It's fine. But we need to find a reason as to why you haven't gone to her already."

"You're right." Tate frowns. "But we are going to think this through, come up with a proper plan. I won't have Iara in danger."

"Someone needs to go." Cass's voice breaks into the conversation. "Keziah must be suspicious by now, if she's been calling Iara with no result."

"I'll go." Antoine stands up, and my stomach clenches in fear.

"No." Cass stands as well, facing Antoine calmly. "It's better if I go. I'll tell Keziah that we've bound Iara in the cellar, just as we trapped her. It means you have to stay hidden," she says, turning to Iara, "but it's the only thing she'll believe. And it will keep her away, for a while, at least. Until we work out what to do."

"Are you sure about this?" Connor's face is dark as he watches Cass. "What if Keziah gets into your head?"

"You know she can't, Connor. Not anymore. Not after Harper's blood. Something changed. I can't even hear Keziah anymore, though I can sense her when she is close. She's no danger to me." Cass gives my brother a small smile. "Though you can come with me, if you're so worried."

"No chance you were going without me." Connor smiles grimly. He turns back to us. "Is there anything else you want to tell us?"

"What do you mean?" My heart skips a beat, then starts to thud again. I can't look at Antoine.

"Well—you could start with where you got that stone thing that cut Iara's connection to Keziah." Connor folds his arms and stares at me. "Come on, Harper. I've known you most of your life. I know when you're hiding something."

"I'm not sure it's safe for Harper to tell you," Antoine starts, but I see the darkness gather on Connor's face again and put a restraining hand on Antoine's arm. There's never much distance from violence between the two of them; they may understand one another, but the truce is uneasy at best.

I meet Connor's eyes. "I will tell you," I say. "I'll tell you everything, but you will have questions I can't answer, or not yet, anyway. Please trust me that I will tell you more as I understand it better myself."

"You mean something more than the fact that you're pregnant by a vampire," says Connor flatly. "As if that wasn't enough."

"Oh," I say, straining for a light tone, "not even close to being enough. I'm pregnant with twins." That shocks them into silence. "And there's more." I take a deep breath. "The twins can time travel. And today is the second time they've taken me with them."

CHAPTER 17

CYPRESS

It's late at night by the time the questions die down and the mansion finally empties out, except for Tate and Iara. Now that Iara is staying here, I suspect we will be seeing a lot more of Tate. I also think that makes Antoine happier than he likes to admit.

Jeremiah is back at the river house, and Callie, as usual, is with him. The subtle undercurrent I felt between them months ago is beginning to surface, but so far, I suspect it is only acknowledged by Callie. The entire time I answered questions about the twins and time travel, Jeremiah was watching Avery, and Callie was watching Jeremiah. I wonder, not for the first time, how that triangle will play out—or if any of the players even understand they are in a game. Despite her best efforts to repair our friendship, Avery is still angry. At me, at Remy, at the world. I wish I knew how to make it better for her.

Antoine and I are in the bedroom. "What are you thinking of?" Antoine's arms wrap around me, and I lean back against him. My body is sagging with the now-familiar aftermath of time travel, exhausted and limp.

"I was thinking of Jeremiah and Avery. And Callie."

"Not to mention Remy." Low laughter rumbles against my back. "It's a complicated knot." His lips touch my neck, making me shiver. "Are you sure that's all you're thinking about?"

"Not really." I pause. "I guess it's more what I'm trying *not* to think about that's the problem."

"Connor?"

"You noticed, huh?"

"The way his face closed over the moment you mentioned Tessa's name? It was kind of hard to miss." His arms tighten around me. "He and Cass left before you could talk to him, didn't they?"

"They said they wanted to get to Keziah before she started wondering why Iara wasn't answering her call. But I saw Connor's face. This is just one more betrayal to him, I think. One more traumatic thing he has to deal with. Connor adored Tessa, just as much as I did. I can't imagine how it must feel to know I've seen her again, had a chance to say goodbye, when he never will."

"Connor loves you. I'm sure you'll find a way to talk it through."

"I hope so." I turn in his arms and he lifts me, carrying me easily to the bed and laying me down. My eyelids are already starting to close. "What are you doing?" I say sleepily, as he lies beside me, still fully clothed. "Come to bed." I reach for him and he chuckles softly.

"I'll stay until you fall asleep." His words are coming through a rapidly falling mist, the soft touch of his finger stroking my cheek urging me toward oblivion. "But then," I hear him say, "I have a wedding to plan."

With a superhuman effort, I raise one eyelid just enough to see him watching me. "Wedding?"

"You said that according to Tessa, you and I are still—in existence, in the future. For long enough to actually raise our children, at least."

"Hm," I manage, my eyelid drooping again.

"You and I might already be married, but I think it's time we made it public." Now his voice is fading, coming down a long tunnel, but I can still hear the laughter in it when he says, "It may well be that a wedding is the only normal thing we ever manage to give our children."

WHEN I WAKE THE NEXT MORNING, NEITHER ANTOINE NOR TATE are home. Iara is cooking, some wonderful slow stew that wafts through the mansion like a comforting blanket. "Cass found Keziah," she says softly, without turning from the pot she is stirring. "She says for now, Keziah believes me to be trapped in your cellar, like she was."

"Is Cass still here?"

"No. She has gone to help Antoine."

"Help Antoine do what?"

Iara shoots me a mischievous look. "You are to be married, no?"

"We are already married."

"*Si*. But I think now, your Antoine makes the big wedding."

"Seriously?" I feel slightly apprehensive. "Cass is helping Antoine organize our wedding?"

"*Si*. But your brother, he is here." She nods down the slope and I'm relieved to see Connor's tall figure out on the jetty. If he's still here, wedding arrangements can't be getting too out of hand. Relief turns to concern as I notice how silent and still he is, staring out over the water. "I think he is not happy," Iara says quietly. "But also that he does not know how to say this."

"I think you're right." I touch her briefly on the shoulder as I pass.

The morning air is soft and scented, still full of summer magnolias. The grass is damp with night moisture, the breeze barely stirring the moss-covered oaks. I pad quietly through the grass, until Connor is barely twenty paces away.

"What did you talk about?" His words are heavy with pain, and I stop in my tracks, unwilling to go closer and interrupt his peace. "When you told the story last night, you mentioned all the things Tessa told you about time pathways and your twins visiting her. But you didn't say what you really talked about, between yourselves." He swings around to face me, and the emotion in his eyes is so raw and open it's all I can do not to reach out to him; something tells me that right now, Connor is the closest to his wolf self that he can be as a man, barely holding on to his human form. His fists clench. "How is it that she never said a word about this? If not to you—at least to me?"

"Oh, Connor." I reach out then, seeing his fists tighten, let my hand drop. "We would never have believed her. Not then. Not even you would have believed her. We'd have thought it was the pain medication, or simply a delusion to take her away from the pain. Tessa had kept the twins a secret for most of her life. Maybe, if future me hadn't turned up, she might have said something in those last days. But not once she'd seen me, after we'd spoken. I think, too, though I don't quite understand it, that the twins warned Tessa about what she could and couldn't say."

"And when you went back in time and saw her, it never occurred to you to ask about anyone else?" His voice is low and angry, his eyes burning as he looks at me. "About Cass, or me? Did you ask her—" his voice breaks. He clears his throat and when he continues, his tone is rusty as old metal, filled with pain. "Did she say how long I would live, Harper?" He reads my face for a moment and his eyes harden. "Did you ask her about anything, except your own life?"

Guilt squeezes the air from my lungs, drains the blood from my face. "I told her that you needed her, as much as I do." My voice is no more than a whisper. "She said that when we talk to her, she really does hear us, Connor. That was the thing she was allowed to tell us both—that she can hear us, even now."

"What does that even mean, if she can't talk back?" Connor throws the words at me like stones. "What use is that to me?"

I step closer, ignoring his ferocious expression, the taut anger in every line of his body. "Tessa said there is a place you go when you want to talk to her. That sometimes you hear her whisper back. She mentioned that there's a certain—plant?" I say the last word uncertainly, worried that any mention of plant magic will be enough to enflame his anger once more. Instead, his face goes oddly still, thoughts like clouds shifting across his eyes.

"The bayou cypress." His eyes stare straight through me, as if he's looking at something beyond me. "Ever since the night I was turned, the bayou is the only place I feel truly safe. When I get down among the swamp cypress, there is a stillness there, as if the whole world is listening."

"And that's where you talk to Tessa?"

"When I'm wolf." His eyes shift back into focus and find mine. "When I'm in the swamp as a wolf, I feel as if I can hear her, feel her, all around me. Even the scent of the cypress reminds me of her, of those last days in the hospital—"

"That's it." I cut him off, gripping his arm in my excitement. "That's what I smelled, when I opened the drawer in her room."

"What?" Connor frowns at me, still wary.

"Cypress. I opened the drawer to get out the figurine for Iara, and I smelled something familiar, but I couldn't quite place where I knew the scent from, or what it was. But that was it—swamp cypress. It smelled like the bayou."

"I brought her back leaves and flowers after I came here to look at the mansion, the first time." Connor is staring at me, excitement lifting his own voice. "We pressed them, together, Tessa and me. In the bible Mom left us."

"That Tessa always kept in the drawer."

He nods, slowly. "And when you gave me that small canister of her ashes, that's where I put them. In the bayou."

"She's there, Connor." I take his hands and look at him, pretending not to notice the tears he is furiously blinking away. "She can hear you. It was the one thing she made me promise to tell you: that when you go to the bayou and talk to her, she's there. She's listening. And when you hear her, it isn't your imagination." I squeeze his hands. "After all we've seen," I say gently, "do you really doubt this? The twins' magic, mine—it all works through water. And you put Tessa's ashes in the water where you speak to her. Of course she's there."

He swallows, and when he speaks his voice is hoarse and strained. "I guess I just wish that I could—that I—"

"That you could say goodbye?"

He nods, unable to speak.

"I said it for both of us." Now my tears are falling, too. "I told her we both knew she had to go, and that afterward, we wished we'd told her. I told her it was okay to let go, to leave us. That we'd never forget her."

"She never cried." Connor's voice is a hoarse whisper. "Not once. I wanted her to cry, to show us she was scared, but all she did was comfort us instead."

"That's because she cried with me." I give him a watery smile. "I held her, told her we would both be there until the end, that her ending would be peaceful. That's why she never showed us her fear, Connor. She'd already cried it out."

My brother's hands are warm in mine. He puts his head back and lets his breath out in a fierce exhale, then draws the clear air in like a benediction. When he meets my eyes again the anger is gone from his. "I'm so glad you could be there," he says simply. "To tell her that."

"And now you need to go and tell her yourself," I say. "She's waiting for you, Connor. I'm sure of it."

His mouth curls up at the corners. "I think she is," he says softly.

I look up at the clear summer sky, then smile at him. "It's a nice day for a run."

"Yes." He looks at me, a hint of his old mischief in his eyes. "Yes, it is. And by the way, if you knew what your husband is planning, you'd be running with me." Before I can make him explain, he is leaping into the air, sending his clothes flying in a spray of ragged material, transforming before my eyes, until a moment later, a sleek, black wolf stands before me on the jetty.

I raise my eyebrows. "Neat trick."

The wolf puts its head to one side, and I can't be sure, but I'm almost certain it winks at me.

Then it bounds away, into the woods along the river, and my brother is gone, into the bayou, to talk with his sister.

CHAPTER 18

DRESS

My Mustang pulls into Deepwater Main Street later that morning. Any hopes I might have had that Connor was just joking with me are dispelled in short order when Jared Baudelaire materializes in front of me on the sidewalk, his face surly. "A friend of mine works at the printer's in Natchez."

"Good for them." I move to go around him, and he blocks my path.

"She called to ask if I wanted a date to the wedding."

"Have fun."

"I asked why on earth I'd be going to a wedding." He glares at me. "Apparently it turns out that not only is it yours, it's also looking like the biggest event on Deepwater's social calendar." He makes a frustrated gesture, oblivious to my shock, and points to the emerald on my left hand. "Wow, Harper. We might not be close, but I don't see why you had to lie and say that rock you've been wearing all year was some kind of family heirloom." He shakes his head. "And Antoine Marigny? Seriously, Harper. He doesn't even have a job."

I bite my lip hard. "His business is all online."

"Sure." Jared rolls his eyes. "Whatever."

His reaction is only the beginning. By the time I've finished grocery shopping, I've been stopped half a dozen times in every aisle. It turns out that Antoine has invited the entire senior class. Tate has added most of the staff to the list. Even Connor must be complicit, since it seems the Legacy Committee families are also invited. Deepwater is full of hushed whispers and curious eyes. Most linger way too long on my belly, although nobody asks me outright if I'm pregnant until Miss Calhoun, the sweet, bohemian art teacher I haven't seen since school finished, corners me in the Blues and Bagels cafe.

"Harper." She nods her head in what she probably thinks is a discreet invitation to sit at her corner table. I planned on grabbing a juice to go, but it seems rude to refuse. An entire room of curious eyes follow my every step as she solicitously pulls my chair out. Miss Calhoun clears her throat uncomfortably. "Tate —that is, Mr. Garrison—gave all the staff invitations to your wedding next week."

Next week? I swallow hard on my shock, vowing to murder Antoine when I get home.

"I have to say I was a little surprised."

Oh, you think you're surprised. I strive to maintain a calm smile and say nothing. I don't trust myself not to swear.

"Harper, I know that you aren't my student anymore, and this may seem like overreach." Miss Calhoun is looking at me with such earnest goodwill that I start to color uncomfortably. "But I happen to believe that art speaks more than words ever can. And I've seen so much in your art, Harper. I feel like I know you in ways others perhaps don't." Despite myself, I can't help but feel touched. "I've been carrying this with me since Tate gave me the invitation, hoping I might find a moment to have a word." She reaches into her bag and holds up a charcoal sketch, and now she has my full attention.

I remember drawing it, the first night I met Antoine on the jetty. I'd sketched his face as I saw it then, as I had felt it. The portrait is grim and forbidding, a shadow of something dangerous lurking behind his eyes. I see in it the stark loneliness he lived before we became what we are to one another. It is a bittersweet thrill to hold it, a reminder of a time when all I knew was what he let me see, a time before I knew both the blazing glory and dangerous darkness of all we are together.

Miss Calhoun leans forward and grips my hands. Too late, I realize she has misinterpreted the emotion in my face. "You don't have to do this, Harper," she says earnestly. "If you need another way out, I can help you. There are . . . alternatives." When I start to shake my head, her grip in my hands tightens. "That portrait speaks volumes. You're scared of him, Harper. Terrified, even. I can't bear to see you marry someone like that. You're not the first girl to . . . get herself in trouble. Please let me help you."

I look down at our joined hands, emotion rising in me with unexpected force, so that when I finally raise my eyes to hers, I realize they are brimming with tears. "Miss Calhoun." She pinches her lips and frowns sympathetically. "I need you to know—" My voice trembles a little. I take a deep breath. "I've never felt happier than I do right now."

I hold her eyes, allowing her to see the deep, profound joy I'm accustomed to keeping guarded from sight. The teacher searches my face closely, and gradually the concern fades from her eyes, slowly replaced by a growing excitement. "Then you mean it's real," she breathes, her eyes shining. Miss Calhoun is an art teacher. At heart, she is a desperate romantic. "That ring you've been wearing. It's truly his?" She holds my hand up in her own and stares at it longingly. "You mean he actually proposed to you before he knew you were pregnant?" When I raise my eyebrows, she shrugs, smiling. "Harper. Deepwater is a small town. Your ultrasound nurse is married to the school secretary. Everyone knows you're expecting twins."

I smother a laugh. "Well, it seems Deepwater isn't quite so well informed as people might like to think." It's Miss Calhoun's turn to raise her eyebrows, but I don't care. If Antoine is sending out wedding invitations, I figure he can just deal with me creating a little havoc of my own. "The truth is," I say in an undertone that has Miss Calhoun hanging breathlessly on my every word, "Antoine and I were married in secret, almost a year ago now. You can search it in the county records. This wedding is just our way of making it public." Feeling an entirely inappropriate satisfaction at her wide-eyed shock, I wink at her. "But I know you'll keep that to yourself."

Absolutely certain there is no way Miss Calhoun will keep that piece of knowledge to herself, I stand up and smile around at the curious faces that all hurriedly pretend they aren't hanging on every word of our conversation. "I hope to see you all this weekend," I say, smiling around at the cafe.

I walk away from their fascinated stares, wishing I actually meant it.

Jeremiah and Callie find me on the sidewalk, frowning at the grocery sacks in the back seat of the Mustang. "We could have done that for you," Callie says.

"I'm fine, truly." I've begun to realize that I'm rarely without an escort of some kind. Avery is waiting by my car. Jeremiah's eyes linger on her just a moment too long then duck away, as if he's ashamed of himself, a faint flush staining his cheeks. Callie's mouth tightens almost imperceptibly. She hugs her bag close to her chest, and I get the feeling that it's through sheer effort of will that she manages to greet Avery civilly. Avery, as usual, is utterly oblivious to the undercurrents. Her eyes are on me, and while she isn't exactly smiling, her expression seems slightly less hostile than it has been the last few times we've met.

"You're coming with me," she says by way of greeting.

"Coming with you where?"

"Shopping." She folds her arms, as if in anticipation of an argument. "In Natchez. Cass is coming, too. She's going to meet us there." Her eyes touch on Callie and harden. "I guess you can come, too. If you want."

"No. Thanks anyway." Callie's response is equally sharp. "Antoine asked Jeremiah and me to help him back home."

Avery shrugs. "Suit yourself."

"Come on." Callie nudges Jeremiah. "We can take those groceries back to the mansion for her."

"Sure." Jeremiah shuffles his feet awkwardly, glancing sideways at Avery. Yet again, she seems oblivious. They lift the sacks out and put them in the white van. Callie gets into the driver's seat, and Jeremiah closes the door behind her then steps back. "I'll meet you there." Jeremiah walks away, thin shoulders hunched over as if to protect his heart from Avery's indifference, as oblivious to Callie's hurt expression as Avery has always been of his. Callie backs out, her little figure stiff-backed and proud in the driver's seat.

I sigh. I wish there was more I could do to help that situation.

"What are we shopping for?" I ask Avery. She's already climbing into the passenger seat of my Mustang and rolls her eyes as she pulls the door closed.

"Your wedding dress, idiot."

I stop in the act of opening the car door and stare at her in open-mouthed astonishment. "You can't be serious."

"As a heart attack." Avery nods at the driver's seat. "Get in. Although maybe I should drive, given your condition."

That snaps me out of my shock. "I am perfectly fine to drive, thank you." Shaking my head, I turn the key and the engine roars into life. "There's no need for all this," I mumble. "We're already married, for goodness' sake."

"And you didn't dress properly for that one. I won't be letting that happen again."

"I was dressed just fine." In fact, even the memory of that day makes my heart clench. Everything about it had been perfect. Everything. I'm not sure that I actually want to get married again. In my mind, that day in the small church, when it was just Antoine and me, will always be our true wedding, no matter the events that occurred after it.

"Well, this time the entire town will be watching, so we need to make sure you do it right."

"Watching my belly, you mean." I put a hand over it protectively, then pull it away again, no wanting to upset Avery.

"It's okay." I glance sideways to find her staring straight ahead. Her face is set, but although I can hear pain in her voice, I don't hear anger or resentment. "I mean, it's okay that all this is happening. You shouldn't have to hide anything from me. It's just that it isn't easy, you know? Not for me—or for Cass, either. Remy won't be with me because he's terrified I'll get pregnant with a wolf, or something even worse, given the whole spirits thing I have going on. Cass won't ever have a baby, no matter what she does. It's just a closed door for her. So, I know it seems like we're the worst friends in the world. I guess I just want you to know that we don't . . . blame you." She casts me a half smile. "We've all ended up dealing with things we didn't expect. You more than anyone, I guess."

"Thank you." I barely manage to croak the word. "And I really do understand how hard this must be. I'm so sorry, Avery. I wish it were different."

"I know." She gives me that same small smile that breaks my heart. I'm glad the top is down on the convertible. The wind dries the moisture on my cheeks before she has a chance to see it. I clear my throat under cover of changing gears. "So, about Remy." It's easiest to change the subject. "Are you two really not talking, then? At all?"

"Not a word since he ditched me. He won't even answer my texts. I guess at least I can go away to college without worrying about when the weird long-distance thing will break us up. He's already cut the cord, so to speak." Despite her levity, there's no humor in her voice, just hollow loneliness, and my heart aches for her. I know how it feels to have someone make decisions about your heart without consulting you.

"Maybe he'll come to the wedding."

"Maybe."

I know I should leave matters there, but then I remember Jeremiah's face, and Callie's tight mouth, and before I know what I'm doing, the words just blurt out of my mouth. "Avery—about Jeremiah."

"What about Jeremiah?"

If I didn't know already, her tone of utter disinterest tells me all I need to carry on. "Jeremiah has got a serious thing for you, Avery. And not just some crush, either."

"It's nothing." She waves a hand dismissively. "Jeremiah and I are just friends. He's a teenage boy, Harper. They're all like that."

"Well, even so. The thing is, I think Callie really likes him."

Avery snorts. "And that's my problem why, exactly?"

I restrain the urge to shake her. "Because as long as Jeremiah thinks he has a chance with you, he won't see what is right in front of him."

"Maybe he sees it just fine but doesn't want it. Callie isn't exactly girlfriend material." Sometimes, I think, Avery can be really hard to like. Some of that thought must be obvious on my face, because Avery sits back and folds her arms. "Fine," she says, glaring at me. "I'll make sure I don't lead him on."

"Thank you."

She casts her eyes skywards. "You're welcome," she says sarcastically. The uncomfortable silence in the car makes me glad when, after following Avery's directions, we pull up in Natchez outside a dress shop and find Cass's long, lean figure propped against her car right outside. In the minute it takes me to park, at least three men almost fall over their own feet trying not to stare at her. Cass ignores them, but I know her, and I can see the faint unease behind her eyes. Somehow, that self-aware-ness is comforting to me. The old Cass would have hated being stared at. The Cass who had been lost for so long had reveled in it. This Cass seems more like a blend of old and new—comfort-able in her new, stunning form, but also humble enough to dislike the effect it has on others. I can't help but remember the last time it was just the two of us: when she learned of my preg-nancy and fled in tears from the garden. Since then, all our communication has been indirect, with others present, and I don't think Cass has actually met my eyes once. She does now, but there is a long way between the wary smile she gives me and the friend I once knew.

"Are you really sure you want to do this?" I ask tentatively as she goes to open the door for me.

"Absolutely." Cass's firm tone belies the wariness in her eyes. "Has it occurred to you that if you don't have a wedding, you will have no wedding photos? What on earth will your twins think of you, when they are old enough to start asking questions?"

"Exactly." Avery steers me inside. "And it's not like we have any good, juicy stories to tell them. At least we can talk about how we made you buy a wedding dress."

"I don't want a traditional wedding dress," I protest, as the bell jangles overhead.

"We figured." Avery points at the racks that stand against each wall, above warm, polished floorboards, but I'm not looking at the dresses. In the center of the floor is a large stone table, topped by a dramatic flower arrangement that reminds me, somehow, of my own wedding bouquet: amaranthus and dusky rose, gray-green leaves amid small buds of something I can't quite place. It's wild and beautiful. "Harper," says Cass somewhat impatiently. "We're not here for the flowers." I finally follow the direction of Avery's finger and can't suppress a gasp of surprise.

"Told you," says Avery smugly.

On one wall there are traditional wedding dresses, the usual insipid shades of cream, ivory, and white, ruched and embroidered and all the meringue confections and fitted sheaths I've seen in bridal magazines. But on the back wall, where Avery is pointing, there is a whole other selection, and these are quite different.

They are made from fabrics that can only be described as works of art. One has a bodice done in cerulean blue and cream that shows a medieval castle around the bust, with a cobblestoned alleyway winding down and around the waistline. Another is designed from fabric made to look like pages of sheet music, cleverly stitched together to create a layered symphony, in colors of old parchment and bronze ink. Yet another looks like antique book covers. Each dress is exquisitely cut and seems to tell a story.

But it's a dress that is hanging from a separate rack that makes me stop and stare.

"I knew it!" Avery casts Cass a triumphant glance as she sees where my gaze rests.

All I can think is that it is my night garden, brought to life in a dress.

The fabric is rich indigo at the bottom hem. As it comes up, the color transforms into emerald, like a summer night over my garden, fading to a sheer pale green at the top. But it is the bodice that makes my heart seize.

It's a moonscape, as if the artist is standing slightly hidden behind delicate sprays of jasmine. The full moon beams down on the dappled surface, and from either side the jasmine creates the feeling of a secret wonderland glimpsed from the shore. The interplay of silver, indigo, and faded green, combined with the imagery and textured effects, are ethereal, like the cover from a fantasy novel. I feel as if by stepping into the dress, I would become part of the scene itself, lost in a dreamscape. The dress is a visual representation of the way I have felt ever since that first day I saw Antoine on the jetty by the river and had my first glimpse of the rich, hidden world hiding beneath the mundane one I knew. It is also eerily reminiscent of the dream I had fore-telling my pregnancy.

"It's magical," I breathe.

Avery nods in satisfaction. "I know, right?"

"Who makes these?"

"A designer in Paris, Sylvie Facon. They are beautiful, *non?*" I've been so consumed by the dress that I barely registered the elegant owner standing off to one side, smiling from beneath an immaculate coiffure. "I am Solange." She has a pronounced French accent. She gestures to the dress I'm admiring. "This dress was made just for you. It came with instructions on how to find you." She nods at Avery, smiling. "I follow the instruc-tions, *et voila.*" She shrugs. "Here you are, and I will fit your dress exactly for you. Although"—she looks me critically up and down—"I am thinking this dress is already perfect."

"Made for me?" I step forward, almost scared to touch some-thing so perfect. "But how is it that this dressmaker—"

"—Sylvie Facon," supplies Solange helpfully.

"Yes. Sylvie. How did she know to make this for me?"

"Ah." Solange gives another elegant shrug. "This, I do not know. I know only that I was sent from the boutique in Paris in which I work to open this shop, just for a time, you understand; it is a, how do you call it, 'pop-up shop'? *Oui.*" Her eyes become momentarily unfocused. Then she seems to mentally shake herself. "*Comme ça*, this dress, it came with me, and now here we are."

I look at Cass and Avery, the unfocused eyes giving me a good idea of who—or what—might lie behind the mystery. "Did Antoine do this?"

Avery shrugs. "I honestly have no idea. Solange called me, so I came to look at the gown. It was perfect, I thought. And here we are."

"But . . ." I want to say that I think Solange has been compelled, but she's a little too close, so I cover by saying, "It's not just a dress. It's a work of art." Somewhat belatedly, I register the chandelier above, the glass fridge holding bottles of Veuve Clicquot and designer chocolates. "How much . . . ?" I let my voice trail off awkwardly, bracing for what I'm sure is about to be an absolutely horrific amount.

"The dress is already paid for." I'm starting to understand the term *Gallic shrug*. Every sentence of Solange's seems punctuated with one.

I frown. "I'm not sure I'm comfortable taking such an expensive gift."

Cass steps forward, waving a black credit card with Antoine's name on it. "Not the issue. Your husband instructed me to use it until, and I quote, *it wears out*."

"I can't—"

Avery steps forward on my other side. "Oh, yes, you can. And you will. As well as shoes, lingerie, and the entire bridezilla nightmare." She turns to Solange. "Let's open some of that champagne. The chocolates too. We're going to be here for a quite a while. Oh, wait." She gives me a slightly evil grin. "We'll only need two glasses. Our bride has passengers on board."

"Wow," I say. "Nasty."

"Oh, yeah." Avery raises her crystal champagne flute and

clinks glasses with Cass, whose smile is equally wicked. "You might get the wedding and the babies. But Cass and I are Veuve, all the way. And we plan to rub it in. At every. Single. Opportunity." Cackling in delight, my two friends collapse on the brocade chaise longue, taking the bottle with them. "Have at it, Solange," Cass says agreeably. "We're in no rush."

LOVE

That evening I stand on the back veranda staring down the slope, where preparations are clearly well underway for the wedding I didn't know was happening. I can't make much sense of it, other than a load of odd shapes in the dusk gloom, but even inside the mansion I can see evidence of frantic work. There's an atmosphere of excitement in the air that I can't help feeling touched by. And every time I allow myself to imagine the exquisite fantasy that is my dress, I actually shiver. Only a few hours earlier I hadn't imagined I could possibly feel excited about doing this, and in public, too; but now, somehow, I am.

I feel the comforting warmth of Antoine's arms slip around my waist.

"When exactly is this wedding happening?" I ask, my lips twitching despite myself.

"Saturday."

I gulp. "As in, less than a week away?"

"In the evening. You don't have to worry about anything. Cass and Avery will take care of you until then. Everyone you know is coming. All the catering and decorating has been sorted out. Iara and Callie are doing most of it. And the same priest who married us will . . . well, he'll marry us again."

"What do you mean when you say that Cass and Avery will look after me?"

"You're going to stay with Cass and Connor tomorrow. No." He shakes his head as I start to protest. "I want you far away from all this. It's going to be madness here. You don't need the stress. And I believe that Cass has found a particularly nice spa for you to relax in for at least two of those days."

I feel like I should be horrified, but somehow I'm just not. Instead, I turn in Antoine's arms, meeting his look of mild trepidation. "I may have added a minor complication to your carefully laid plans."

He raises his eyebrows. "Oh?"

"Uh huh." I entwine my arms about his neck. "News of our pregnancy seems to have made its way into gen pop, so I told Miss Calhoun that you married me last fall." Giving him a wide-eyed, innocent smile, I say sweetly, "Given your obvious powers of compulsion, I'm sure there's nothing there you can't handle?"

I take an inordinate amount of pleasure in watching the shifting expressions move across his face. First comes the concentrated expression as he tries to remember what he's told people, closely followed by consternation as he tries to track the lies he's told. But my greatest satisfaction comes when I see the gray shade of stress that comes over his face as he tries to work out how to manage my little bombshell.

"Have fun with that," I say, patting him on the arm. "As much fun as I had, going to town to discover you'd organized our entire wedding."

He catches my arm as I go to walk away, his face suddenly dark with worry. "Harper. I didn't mean to upset you. I know how much you hate fuss. I wanted to save you the stress . . ."

I let his voice trail off and give him a few moments to squirm in embarrassment before I can't take it anymore. I burst into laughter. "Thank goodness you did. If I'd had to organize this kind of thing, we'd all be waiting until the end of days." He looks up at my face, unsure if I'm really joking until he sees my expression, and his own finally relaxes.

"I honestly thought I'd messed up." He kisses me.

"I stopped being annoyed after I saw that amazing dress." I link my hands behind his neck and pull him closer. "How in the world did you find time to do that?"

"Dress?" His eyes narrow slightly. "I didn't have anything to do with a dress."

"Oh, you mean you didn't go to Paris, have a designer named Sylvie Facon make my dream dress, and compel a lady named Solange to bring it over to me?"

It's only when I see the complete bemusement in his face that a faint unease takes hold. "You were the one who did that, weren't you?"

"No." He meets my eyes. "No, Harper. I didn't do that."

I step back from him, the unease growing. "Then who did?"

"I truly don't know." He is frowning now. "But I'll find out, Harper. I promise you that."

THE FOLLOWING MORNING, I'M PACKING A BAG TO TAKE TO CASS'S and trying not to think about the mysterious origins of my beautiful dress, when Callie comes in and perches on my bed, picking at the eiderdown in a way that makes it clear she has something on her mind. I keep packing, well aware that Callie talks in her own time.

"So, Jem'll be goin' on to college next week."

Alarm bells scream at the sudden reappearance of Callie's Memphis tough talk.

"Uh huh." I keep folding clothes, keeping my tone carefully neutral.

"Asked me if I'd drive his stuff on down to Oxford in the van, so he can ride that bike of his."

"Sure. Sounds logical."

"Don' know as I'll do it, or no."

"Okay," I say carefully, aware she is watching me closely. "Why is that?"

"Tol' me he wants to take Avery's stuff in the van, too. Whatever won't fit into that cutesy little hatchback o' hers." Callie's tone makes her disdain at Jeremiah's request, Avery's stuff, and the offending hatchback abundantly clear.

"Ah."

"Yeah." After a short silence, she goes on. "I'm not sayin' as I don' like Avery. I'm sure she's nice. But she's one o' those girls, you know? Nice family, nice house, so pretty every guy wants to date her. She could have anyone she wants, but she just can't help herself playin' with Jem. Even though she ain't *never* actually gonna be with him."

I think of Avery's parents, both part Natchez, who have worked their entire lives to lift themselves out of the disadvantage they were raised with, and who want more than anything to see Avery succeed without the same struggle they faced. "People's lives aren't always what they look like from the outside, Callie. From what I understand, Avery's parents were both raised in the bayous, passed between family members, often with drug and alcohol problems. They both won scholarships to college on their own merit. They've worked incredibly hard to make sure Avery doesn't face the same difficulties they did. Remy . . . represents everything they are the most afraid of, and Avery knows that. Jeremiah, on the other hand, is the kind of boy they'd love to see Avery be friends with."

"So you're sayin' Avery's friends with Jeremiah to keep her parents happy? How is that fair?"

"It isn't fair at all, but I don't think that is all it is. In her own way, Avery is every bit as lost as anyone else. Maybe subconsciously, she needs a friend as much as you do. And you of all people know what a good friend Jeremiah can be."

"But Jeremiah doesn't see her as a friend. And she's going to hurt him." The hard accent is gone, her voice fragile with hurt.

"Perhaps." I sit on the bed beside her. "But you can't control that either, Callie, or protect Jeremiah from being hurt. All you can do is decide whether you can be his friend, or not."

"He's the best friend I've ever had." She puts her head on my shoulder. It's such an oddly vulnerable gesture it makes my heart clench.

"I know that." I stroke her hair gently. "And if you really mean that, you will be there for him. Because if you're right, and he does get hurt, he'll need a friend more than ever."

"I'm scared of saying goodbye to him." Her voice is muffled, and I'm fairly sure she's trying not to cry. "And of being here all alone next year, especially when you have the twins."

"You won't be alone. Antoine and I will be here, and Iara, too. Who also, incidentally, needs a friend." Callie pulls away, swiping at her eyes, and I smile at her. "From what I've seen, being a friend is something you're pretty good at."

"I guess." Nodding and sniffing, she stands up. "I'll tell Jeremiah I'll drive the van, then. And take Avery's stuff."

"Good for you." I look critically at the bag on the bed that I've just been packing. "Speaking of stuff, I have absolutely no idea what to pack for this week."

Callie beams. "I can help with that. I know everything you're going to be doing."

"Of course you do," I say dryly, but the irony is lost on her, and the next hour is spent in a whirlwind of clothes and bags and organization. By the time Callie is finished, the Mustang is loaded with more clothes than I imagine needing for a year, let alone a few days, and I'm feeling rather bewildered as Antoine comes outside to say goodbye.

"I really won't see you all week?" I shake my head. "That feels like a long time."

"It's also better this way. By the time you come back, everything will look different."

"I'm not sure if that's a good thing or not." I look around at the peeling plaster, the half-cut pieces of wood and general dilapidation. "I kind of like it like this."

"It won't be that different." Antoine smiles, his arms sliding around my waist. "I'm a vampire, not a wizard. Even I can't finish the entire renovation in a matter of days. We're just going to make it a little more . . . presentable."

"And protected, I imagine?" I look up at him, and his eyes glow with the cobalt and gold that always makes my heart flip.

"Protected, yes. Lori and Avery are going to work with Iara to make sure we don't have any unwanted visitors the night of the wedding." His hands tighten momentarily against my back.

"Do you think Keziah will come back?" I don't want to ask the question. Speaking her name feels like inviting her in. It sends a shudder down my back, but it's also empowering. Somehow I don't want to avoid talking about her, as if she's some kind of shadow lurking around every corner. I want to reduce her to a problem to be solved.

"I don't think she's given up, if that's what you're asking. She knows you're pregnant, Harper. That means she's going to come back. Keep coming back. Until we find a way to end her for good." He tucks a curl behind my ear, his thumb tracing my jaw. "Keziah believes we've worked out how to activate the binding at will. She believes—or at least, Cass told her—that should she step on this land again, land your nature power is tied to, that she, too, can be bound once more. For all Keziah's ambition, three centuries locked in a cellar is a powerful deterrent. And besides, there's nothing she can actually do until the twins are born. I don't think she'll risk harming you."

"But after they're born . . ." I look up at him, unwilling to put my fears into words.

He holds my face, his big hands comforting. "We're going to find a way to end Keziah, Harper. We'll keep Iara hidden. Keziah doesn't know Iara is not hers to control. She'll be waiting, planning to regain control over her progeny. When that moment comes, Iara will be the weapon she doesn't see coming. We just have to work out how best to use that weapon."

"Do you truly think Keziah will leave me alone until after the twins are born?"

His mouth tightens into a grim line. "I'll be doing everything in my power to make sure she comes nowhere near any of us until then."

"You don't think . . ." I swallow, trying to find the words for the horrible suspicion that has been chasing my dreams. "You don't think that my dress is some kind of trap she's set for me, do you?"

"Ah." His face breaks into an unguarded smile that is surprising, given the topic of conversation. "The mysterious dress." His smile is so wide it's infectious. "No, trust me. I found the source of the dress. It's definitely surprising, but not at all sinister. Let's just say for now that it's a gift from someone who loves you, and who knows you very well."

"You know who made it? Tell me!" I rear back and try to examine his eyes, but he wards me off, laughing.

"It's a secret—one I'm keeping. You'll find out eventually. But it definitely isn't Keziah. Trust me on that."

My curiosity fades, and I press close to him, my cheek against the broad wall of his chest. "I'm scared of her, Antoine. Not for myself. For what she might do to them. To our babies." His arms wrap around me, holding me close, and I want to stay in their warm security forever. "I don't want to go away this week. I want to stay here, with you." Laughter rumbles against my face, and one hand cups my head, stroking my hair softly.

"Connor and Cass will keep you safe until the wedding. The wolves and Connor are on better terms, since he helped them chase Keziah off again. Remy and the pack will be close by, running security. If she gets too close, Cass will sense her and bring you right back here. For now, though, we think she's gone. Possibly to South America, to find out more about Iara, though I can't be sure. None of us can sense her close, not even Iara. So I think, for the time being at least, we're clear." He tilts my face up. "As for the twins," he says gently, "nothing is going to hurt them, Harper. We will all make sure of that. And if nothing else, remember that Tessa said she saw them into their mid twenties."

"But not beyond." It's been bothering me ever since my sister said it. "She never saw them any older than that."

"She also said that was something you would understand in time and had no need to worry about."

"How do I not worry about it?" I shake my head. "And how can I be sure all of that can't change if something goes wrong? Maybe Tessa never saw them at all. Maybe all of that past can change. I don't understand how this works. None of us do. How am I supposed to raise twin girls who can time travel, Antoine?"

He holds my face steady between his hands, and my eyes with his own. "I know, Harper. Okay? I know. Don't think that every night when I go to feed I don't wonder how I am supposed to explain to baby girls that their father has to feed from humans in order to survive. I wish I could tell them that everything was like the movies, that I lived on animals or from blood banks and never harmed a human. I wish I could know that they will be born perfectly normal, like every other human baby. But I can't tell them lies about what I am, just as none of us can truly know what the twins themselves are going to be. Their father is a vampire. Their mother is an Abatey. And we already know they can time travel. None of this is normal, or without danger, or anything that Dr. Spock has written a book to explain. But somehow we're going to find a way through it. And this weekend, Harper, we're going to get married in front of the entire town, like any other normal couple. People are going to gossip about your pregnancy and the fact that we got married in secret while you were underage. We will be everyone's favorite story—until the next one comes along." He kisses me, long and sweet, until my entire body is straining toward his and he pulls away, his eyes glittering darkly. "What I do know is that we are going to love one another, and our babies, with all that we have," he says roughly. "And somehow, that is not only going to be enough, Harper. It's going to be more than enough."

CHAPTER 20

FRIENDS

The week passes in a strange, late-summer haze.

Somewhere between dress fittings, spa treatments, and watching old movies, Cass and I find our way back to a comfortable friendship. I tell her about Tessa and confide my fears about what may lay ahead for the twins. Cass tells me it broke her heart to give up her dream of studying music, but that she's decided to study anyway, with a private tutor. Eventually, she hopes she may be able to face going to college in some way, one day when she and Connor are both more comfortable in their new, supernatural skins.

"For now, it's enough just getting through each day," she says. "People have stopped staring at me quite so much. It's strange what humans will accept as normal. I look completely different than I used to, and I behaved appallingly to people while I was under Keziah's control. But instead of thinking something is wrong, everyone whispers that my mother died suddenly, and that I've just grown up fast. It's like they can't see what is right under their noses—or don't want to." She gives me a slightly sad look. "It's lonely, sometimes. To think I will outlive them all. Have to leave here eventually, when it becomes obvious that I'm not aging. Especially for Connor. I know he wanted to grow old here."

I remember Connor, talking about us both raising children in the mansion, with a bittersweet ache in my heart. Even if Antoine and I can't stay there forever, for the same reasons Cass will one day have to leave, my children will at least walk the hallways of the mansion. But Connor . . . if he stays with Cass, they will never have children. I know how much that upsets her, not just for herself, but for Connor, too.

"I've told him he should leave me." Cass says this from the sink, without looking at me. "I tried to make him go, to find a partner from Remy's pack, or even leave and find another pack to live with. But he won't hear of it." She shakes her head. "Neither of us even knows how long he will live," she says quietly. "I don't know how long we will have together. The legends say that the wolves live longer than other men—but how long, we don't know."

My heart aches for her. "No matter how long my brother has on this earth, I know he would want to spend that time with you." I try to keep my voice steady. "You don't know Connor like I do. He's never been able to truly be himself with someone. He's always been looking after others. His father, Mom, Tessa, me. With you, he's truly himself. It's hard to explain how wonderful it is for me to see. I can only imagine what a gift it is to Connor."

She still doesn't face me, but when she speaks I can hear the emotion in her voice. "For me, too," she says softly. "Being with Connor is the first time I've felt truly myself. I can't imagine life without him. But I also can't believe it, sometimes. It's as if being together is a dream that I might wake up from at any time. Every morning when I wake up, I wonder if I've dreamed the whole thing. Then, when I realize I haven't, I start worrying that he will be taken from me, or that Keziah will kill one of us. Any number of crazy things."

"Not crazy at all." I'm almost laughing, and she finally turns around. "I think the same thing."

"You do?"

I nod. "Every. Day. I was scared to come here for the week, in case I returned to find Antoine, and even the mansion, had disappeared in my absence." I reach into my bag and pull out the ultrasound photo. "I carry this everywhere with me and look at it a hundred times a day, to reassure myself I haven't imagined the whole thing. I write everything down in letters to Tessa, and when I read them, I wonder if I just went crazy. Even when I look at the ring on my finger, I wonder if I didn't just make the story up in my mind. I've always had a creative imagination."

"Seriously?" Cass's face lightens, and for the first time in what seems like forever, she breaks into a real, open-faced smile. "Do you know," she glances around as if she's afraid of being overheard, "sometimes I jump up to the top of a really tall tree. I can do it in one leap, if I try hard. And I perch there, right on the tip of the branch. I do it on my tiptoes, like an angel at the top of a Christmas tree, and I stay there for a long time, without breathing at all. I don't do it because it's a challenge. I do it because sometimes I still need proof of what I've become." She meets my eyes and the light fades a little. "I used to be afraid of feeding," she says quietly. "After all that time with Keziah. I could never stop, when I was with her. And Keziah didn't want me to. She doesn't care about humans, Harper. At all. To her, people are nothing more than a food source, something to play with and then throw away. And in a strange way I can understand that." Seeing my face, she gives me an apologetic half smile. "I know how that must sound. But after a while in this skin, after realizing that I will truly live forever—it's hard to see people the same way, Harper. That's why I was afraid of feeding. I thought I would lose it, like I did with her. But then Antoine and Tate showed me how they do it, and gradually, it got easier."

I bite my lip. "And how is it? I mean, when you . . . feed with them?" Somehow, I don't want to confide that Antoine has rarely spoken about feeding to me. I think I've always known why he doesn't. Even after all this time, and after he's drunk from me, I know he's afraid that the reality of how he survives will make me see him differently. I've always remembered what he said long ago, the night Keziah escaped, before he drank from me. *All the books and movies lie, Harper. We don't shine in the sun. We don't live off animals, or blood banks, or other vampires. We might not need to kill, but we do need human blood to survive.*

"Blood creates a bond," Cass says quietly. "When we take blood from a person, we feel like they do. For a little while, at least, it's almost like we *become* them. With Keziah, she would choose prey because of their strength and aggression. Athletes, fighters. Criminals, even. The more violent, for Keziah, the better."

"But Antoine and Tate aren't like that?"

"No, they aren't. They taught me to find the lonely, the sad, the lost."

I frown. "But when you do that, doesn't it make you feel the same way?"

"There's more to feeding than just the blood, Harper. When we finish, we give some of our own blood back, just enough to heal the wounds we've made, and to strengthen the humans we've drunk from. A little of ours goes a long way. Keziah never gave humans her blood; for her, like I said, humans were playthings. She didn't care how weak she left them. But Antoine and Tate taught me that when I drink, I can also give something back, in the compulsion I use, and with my blood."

I have a sudden recollection of words Antoine once said, when he spoke of feeding: *I found a woman who was sad and tired and had nowhere to go, and then I drank from her. A few hours from now, she will wake to find herself in a cheap motel with fifty dollars she didn't know she had, a little dizziness, and a strange resolution that she never wants to drink alcohol again.*

"You change them for the better."

"Don't make it more than it is, Harper." Cass's voice has a warning note in it, and when I meet her eyes, they are grave, full of regret. "Don't try to make us something good. We're still monsters who drink from others to live. Giving a little of our blood, some compulsion to make someone feel stronger or better about themselves—it's still a dirty bargain for what we take."

"But that's why you seek them out? The lonely, the sad, the lost? You help them to feel better?"

She nods. "When we take their blood, we take some of that feeling into us, and when we give them ours, those emotions are transmuted. They wake not so much changed as . . . understanding themselves better. And for us, their emotion becomes part of us. But so does the cure we give them. It's almost like every feed adds to my understanding of people. Who they are, how they feel. Almost as if I see the world through a different lens, for a while."

"That sounds fascinating." I mean it.

Her eyes darken. "Yes. But dangerous, too. Antoine and Tate have taught me a lot about the need to keep myself separate from those I feed on, not to lose myself in it—not to allow a bond to form where I could control them. After we feed, we compel them to forget us completely. Maybe we help them to heal something in themselves with that compulsion, but we break any attachment they may have to us. Forming bonds with us is dangerous for humans, just as losing ourselves in the feed is for us. When we drain someone completely, to death, it's a dark act, Harper. Those souls stay within us. For years. Longer, even. There are people who I can feel inside me now. And it is a dark feeling. One I often loathe myself for." She breaks off and turns away abruptly, holding her arms protectively across her middle. "I know you love Antoine," she says in a hollow voice. "Just as I love Connor. But I wouldn't want this life for him. And

I'm sure Antoine doesn't want it for you." She turns to look at me over her shoulder. "I understand why you're marrying him, and I'm glad you're having your twins. It's nothing short of a miracle. But have you even discussed what happens later, Harper? After the twins are born? Are you going to become a vampire, too? Can you?"

I swallow. Those questions have haunted me in the nights, particularly since I became pregnant. It's certainly not the first time I've had to face them head-on. I recall Tate, long ago, when we first met: *A human in love with a vampire? After seeing you today, I believe you can imagine that perfectly.*

"I don't know what the future holds, Cass, any more than you do." My voice sounds stronger than I thought it would. "I guess at some point, I've had to stop thinking about what's going to happen and start just living with what *is* happening, every day. Right now there's so much that simply living it is all I can manage."

Cass nods slowly, and gradually her face relaxes. "Maybe that's all any of us can do."

"Maybe."

"So tomorrow is your wedding day, huh?" She shakes her head. "I can't say it's what I imagined doing the summer after we graduated school."

"Oh, you think I did? Not to mention, you know." I point at my belly.

"Well, at least nobody can call it a shotgun wedding, since the whole town seems to know now that you were married a year ago."

"I'm honestly not sure what's worse. A secret, underage elopement or my teenage pregnancy."

Cass laughs. "Oh, come on. A teen pregnancy is hardly news around here. The real irony is that half the attendees at your wedding will be the kind of supernatural that makes your wedding seem like child's play." I can't suppress a shiver.

Cass puts her hand on my shoulder. Her touch is a reminder that Cass is no longer the submissive girl I once knew. Her hand is iron hard, even if the gesture is gentle. "Don't worry, Harper." A savage red gleams behind the mahogany eyes. "Your wedding will be safe. We'll make sure of that."

CHAPTER 21

The night before the wedding, I'm lying fully clothed on the bed when there's a knock on the window. I smile when I see Antoine on the roof outside, leaning on the sill. When I open it, he leaps into the room easily and lounges against the wall, grinning.

"I thought we weren't seeing each other until tomorrow." I sit on the bed.

"I was worried you might be having second thoughts." Antoine settles himself on the window seat and crosses his long legs at the ankle.

"It's about a year too late for second thoughts."

He laughs softly. "I guess so. But I wanted to check." His eyes linger on me, a certain gravity lurking behind the smile. "Word has traveled. Even among our kind, weddings are special. If they're real, that is."

"And this one is real?"

He raises his eyebrows quizzically. "You really need to ask me that?"

I color. "I guess not. It's just that I'm not . . . you know."

"A vampire?"

I nod.

"That doesn't matter to me, Harper. And I'm not the first vampire to marry a human. Those who know will all assume that later . . . well." He cuts off abruptly, frowning.

"That I will become a vampire." I finish the sentence for him. He doesn't say anything, nor does he look at me. "Is that why you came here tonight, Antoine?" I say quietly. "Did you come to ask me that question?" I'm expecting him to look away again or brush off my question, as he does any time I come close to asking about our future. But this time, he doesn't.

"The last time we got married," he says, "it wasn't about the future. It was about keeping you safe and Keziah bound. We never talked about what it would mean for you long-term. For us. I'm not sure I even thought of the long-term, ironic as that sounds, coming from someone who should really be accustomed to long-term planning." I can't help but smile at that. He swings his legs off the window seat and leans forward, clasping his hands loosely between his knees as he looks intently at me. "It's different now," he says in a low voice. "Once we do this tomorrow, it will be public. People, including those of my own kind, will know we're married. There's no going back from this, nor compelling people to forget it happened. Once we stand before the congregation tomorrow, we aren't just married on paper, Harper. We're married forever. And forever, in my world, is a very long time."

His words send a thrill through my body that has nothing to do with wedding jitters. It's something deeper, more potent, than that. "Did you invite any of your—friends?"

"Only one. And Guidry de Ainhoa isn't a vampire. He's a wolf. Or he was." Antoine frowns. "He's lived almost as long as I have. He's never told me how, though, and I've never asked."

"Does he know? About the twins?"

"Yes." It's a simple statement, but one that rocks me to the core nonetheless. For some reason, I had expected him to keep it a secret, to try to protect me.

"Does he know what I am, then, too?"

"In a way." He watches me. "Tate and I have told him you have nature powers, though not the specific nature of those powers."

"Why did you tell him?"

"Because he would have sensed you were pregnant anyway. Guidry has the sharpest senses of anyone I've ever met."

"What did he say? Did he ask questions?" I'm intrigued.

He half smiles. "Guidry isn't much of a talker. But he is a good friend. I promised him once that if I ever married, he'd be there. At the time it was said as a dark joke, but Guidry is one of the few friends I've never lost touch with. If you don't want him to be there, though, just say the word, Harper." His half smile twists a little. "Guidry of all people won't take offense."

"No," I say instantly. "Of course he should come, if he's your friend. But is friendship the only reason you invited him?" I can't shake the feeling that there's more to what he's saying.

"There are times when I wish I could compel you to be less perceptive." Antoine's tone is wry, but he doesn't shy from the question. "Guidry came from this country originally, but he's spent most of his life abroad. He knows many of my kind and is trusted by them. He's a good ally, and he knows many more who could also be allies, if we should need them."

"I thought you said that I would be at risk if they knew? That my blood would make me a target for every vampire?"

"That was exactly what I thought. But Tate sees it differently, and for once, he made me see it his way." He looks up at me cautiously. "The more public we make this, the harder it will be for someone to just take you. For all our bloodthirst, vampires—those who live past the first few decades, at least— have a reverence for life that exceeds anything that humans can begin to understand. We may not mingle with humans, nor share their lives, for the most part. But that isn't because we don't respect them. It's because being among humans is a reminder of everything we ourselves can't have. Remaining separate is a kind of self-preservation, I guess you might call it."

I think of my conversation with Cass a few days ago. "Keziah doesn't feel that way, though, does she." I meet his eyes steadily. "Cass said Keziah despises humans as weak creatures, no more than playthings."

Antoine's mouth hardens and he stands up abruptly. "There are those like Keziah amongst us," he says curtly. "Of course there are. Predators. Evil creatures who think nothing of torturing humans—or each other. At different times, most vampires face that aspect of their nature, become it, at least for a while. I've told you this." I nod. I know he himself has had his own struggles with his nature. "But there are many more of us who are nothing like that," he says quietly. "Who use the decades to learn and grow. Become, if not better, at least the best we can be." He moves restlessly about the room, not looking at me. I can feel his tension. I know that beneath whatever he is saying, there is another conversation to be had.

"Why are you telling me this, Antoine?" I stand up and go over to him, putting my hand on his arm and forcing him to stop, turning him to face me. "Why did you come here tonight?" For a moment I think he won't answer, his face the smooth mask he employs when he wants to hide his thoughts from me. Then he sighs, raking one hand through his hair as if he's thought it through too many times and has forced himself to come to this decision.

"After the twins are born," he says roughly, "after we are sure they are safe, and you too. After we have learned all we can about what you are, and only if we discover it is safe to do so, Harper—" He breaks off and swallows hard.

"Would I consider becoming a vampire?" I say gently. His

eyes fly to my face, startled, but he doesn't say anything. He just nods, watching me. "Yes," I say slowly. "Yes, Antoine, I would."

His eyes widen, then darken. He opens his mouth then closes it again, waiting for me to speak.

"Yesterday I was talking with Cass. I told her that I'd stopped thinking about what was going to happen because I had to just focus on living every day. I realized afterward that isn't true. Or at least, it isn't true anymore." I stare out into the darkness, to the trees visible from Cass's window. It is always like this, with Antoine. My thoughts happen in the depths of my mind, and then he seems to reach inside and pull them to the surface. When he does, what I truly feel rises with them, taking me by surprise.

"Of course I've thought about it. How could I not? I've thought about it, one way or another, almost every day since we've been together." I touch my belly. "Before now, I didn't really want to consider it, because I knew that becoming a vampire would mean no children. No matter what I felt for you, I simply couldn't imagine giving up the possibility of having children. It's too important to me. But now . . . everything is different."

"Different how?" He grasps my hands, his eyes searching my face. "Why? Harper, if you change after this, the twins are the only children you will ever have." His voice breaks off abruptly. He takes a deep breath, and I can tell he's steeling himself to say something. "There's no guarantee they will be born safely," he says hoarsely. "We know nothing of what they are, of what might happen."

"No." I cut him off, unwilling to so much as contemplate the dark visions his words conjure up. "The twins will be born, I'm sure of it, Antoine. There's too much proof they live. But after they're born, they're going to be in danger—and so am I." When I see his face close over, I shake my head impatiently. "There's no point denying it, Antoine, or getting angry. It's a fact. If, or when, the twins are born, every vampire on earth will see them as proof that my blood is magic. They will all want to drink that magic and try to make a child of their own. You said it yourself. Vampires have a reverence for life. Whether they are allies or not, they will see what has happened between us as a miracle. And who wouldn't do anything they could to make a miracle of their own?" I step closer to him, so we are chest to chest, the hard length of his body warm and reassuring against my own. "It's one thing to be a target when it's only me, Antoine. But I won't put our girls in danger. They're going to need two strong parents to defend them, and anything else we can corral into helping us. Wolves, witches—you name it. If it's out there and I can use it, I will, if it means keeping them safe. The first step to doing that is by becoming a vampire myself."

His hands cup my face. "I never wanted this for you," he says roughly.

"I know that. I know if there was any way to do it differently, you would choose it. But there isn't."

"We might still find one."

I know the hope he feels. I've felt it myself, the shaky, thin light of an alternative, glimmering amid the darkness. But something about being pregnant has made me brave enough to look past illusion. The lives I carry are too important to lose because I can't bear to face reality. As much as part of me wants to believe that there is a magical solution out there, a stronger, deeper, more urgent part of me insists that I make plans based on what I know to be true at this moment. I cover Antoine's hands with my own.

"Perhaps between now and then, yes, we might discover something. But what we already know is that from the very moment our girls come into this world, they will be a magnet, attracting not just Keziah, but every vampire on earth who wonders if the twins' blood might hold the same magic mine does. And that means our girls will need me to be not just their mother, Antoine. They will need me to be their protector. I'm not going to risk the lives of the miracles I have already been given by dreaming that I might be granted another one."

Antoine's face looks as if it's been carved from stone, his eyes burning the brilliant gold they do when emotion overtakes him. "Don't you want more time, after they're born, to be sure?"

"No." I shake my head determinedly. "I want them safe, Antoine. You have to believe me. This decision isn't about what I want anymore. It's about what will keep them safe. I can't spend my life depending on you and Tate to protect me, and I can't trust others to protect our daughters. I need to know I can do that myself. And even if I believe the magic in my veins is strong enough to fight off Keziah, so long as I have it, I'm also a target. And so long as I'm a target, I can't be what I need to be for our daughters."

My own breathing is the only sound in the silence that follows, though the frail pulsing of my heart seems deafening inside me. I spoke without consciously planning my words, the thoughts taking shape as I spoke them. But now that they're said, I feel their weight. In saying them aloud, I've made a pact. Not with Antoine necessarily. With myself, with the invisible forces I feel within me and without, with the twins themselves. I have chosen a water path. One that will change everything, forever. I meet Antoine's eyes and see the same realization mirrored in them.

"You will sacrifice yourself, without knowing what will become of the magic in your veins or what manner of creature you might be reborn as?" His thumbs stroke my cheekbones, his eyes moving back and forth over my own. "I can't even bear to think of what might happen, Harper." His voice cracks slightly. "I know it is what we *should* do. That it's the only real solution. But the thought of it terrifies me to the marrow of my bones."

I press his face between my own hands, and his slide down to hold my hips. Though his touch is light, I can feel his tension.

"When we marry tomorrow," I say, "it really is for always, Antoine. The moment our girls are born, I need you to make sure I can be *their* always, too, not just yours. When we make our vows tomorrow, it isn't to bind a spell or even to bind you and me together. It's a vow to our family, the family that we've created together. And the only way to keep that family safe is for you to turn me into a vampire the moment after the girls are born. So whatever it was that you came here to ask me, answer me this instead: tomorrow, when you vow to be bound to me until death do us part, do you accept that you are also promising to not only be the one who causes my death, but the one who ensures I am reborn with our twins—this time into immortality?"

The room is silent. Beyond the window, an owl cries into the night, a strange, hollow sound that hits my spine. I can't see the moon from Cass's house, but I know it is growing, will be full when we marry tomorrow night. The air feels heavy with expectation as I wait for Antoine to speak.

"I need this vow from you, Antoine. Please."

For a while, I think he simply won't answer me, but finally his arms pull me close, my own going around his neck, and I feel the racing thud of his heart against mine. "I married you once without asking that question," he says roughly. "I told myself it was because the marriage would only last until I found a way to break the curse, but that was a lie. I didn't want to ask the question because I was afraid of your answer."

He takes a deep breath. "But I've lived too long to lie, Harper, to myself and especially to you. I couldn't bear for you to marry me again with that question silent between us."

"Me neither." I hadn't realized it until now, standing here in his arms with the unspoken finally laid before us, laid to rest. "I think deep down I've always known where this had to end." I pull back so I can look at him. "No matter what I told myself the last time we married, inside I knew it wasn't because of the binding. Even then, I knew it was more than that."

His eyes gleam, his mouth curling in the half smile that always makes heat rush through my body. "Always," he murmurs.

I nod slowly. "Always."

I sway forward, and then my eyes spring open when I realize he's flown from my embrace. He smiles at me crookedly from the window sill. "Tomorrow night, Mrs. Marigny." This time his eyes positively burn gold. "It's a promise."

And then he's gone, into the moonlit night.

CHAPTER 22

PEARL

The sun is falling to the edge of the horizon, dark storm clouds brewing ominously over the river, when Connor knocks on my door late the following afternoon. I'm standing by the window after what has already felt like a marathon of a day. I had no idea how exhausting wedding preparations could be. I have been styled, made up, and pampered until I barely recognize myself. I'm more nervous than I could have imagined, and Connor is about to be my first test. "Come in." I turn around, my voice trembling despite my best intentions.

Connor pushes open the door and takes a stride inside, then stops in his tracks. His mouth drops partly open as he stares at me. The silence stretches on, until I am entirely unnerved.

"Please say something." I barely recognize my voice. "Your silence is scaring me more than anything else could."

"I don't know what to say," he says slowly. "I'm not sure what I expected. I don't know that I thought about it, really. But this . . . that dress. Harper." He shakes his head in wonder and then, to my vast relief, a slow smile stretches across his face. "You look like a fairy tale," he says softly.

"In a good way, I hope," I say shakily.

"In a very good way." He comes across the room and reaches out, holding my upper arms. "You are . . . extraordinary, Harper." Something in the way he says it makes me think he's talking about more than my dress, and that makes me feel so close to tears I step back and smile brightly.

"You look amazing." I strive for a lighter tone, not wanting to lose it completely. And my brother really does look incredible. His tux highlights the breadth of his shoulders, the lean, hawkish planes of his face.

He grins. "I know." The smile is gone just as quickly, replaced by a warm expression that is so reminiscent of the brother I knew throughout all the hard years that once again tears threaten to crush the back of my throat. "Mom and Tessa would have loved this," he says quietly. "That dress. It's so you, so very different from any normal wedding dress. It looks like your garden come to life."

"Thank you," I manage. I'm finding it hard to speak.

Connor reaches into his jacket and pulls out a small box. "Tessa gave this to me before she died." He's not looking at me, his voice rough, struggling, I suspect, just as much as I am to maintain his composure. "I know Mom gave you the pearl earrings you're wearing." I touch the pearls at my ears. "Mom left Tessa the matching ring," Connor continues. "Before Tessa died, she asked me to give it to you. She told me not to give it to you until the right moment. She said I'd know when it was." He gives me a small smile. "Now is that moment. And I hope you don't mind, but I opened it before I gave it to you. I guess I just wanted to make sure it wouldn't upset you."

I stare down at the ring. I remember it on Mom's finger, a large single pearl set in white gold.

"Look at the inscription on the inside," Connor says.

I do. Engraved in swirling writing is one word: *always.*

A chill goes down my spine. "Did you have that done?" I whisper, staring at it.

"No. It was like this when Tessa gave it to me." Connor's smile is heartbreaking. "But it means something to you, doesn't it?"

I blink back tears. "It's the same word that's on my emerald. And on the inside of Antoine's wedding ring."

Connor's smile deepens, and something glistens in his eyes. "There's more." He reaches into his pocket and pulls out a small, tightly rolled piece of paper. "This was tucked inside the ring. Read it."

I unroll it with trembling hands.

My darling sister,

This is the evening you marry Antoine. I wish, more than anything, that I could be there in person. But because of your extraordinary girls, part of me will be.

I stop reading. "No," I breathe. "It's not possible."

My brother's face is blurry through my tears. "Possible," he says softly. "Keep reading."

Maybe I should have told you of this when we finally met today. Selfishly, I wanted to surprise you. I always said I would design your wedding dress. The girls described your night garden to me, so I could use it as inspiration. I do not have time to sew the dress myself, but I chose the fabrics, touched them with my own hands. The girls tell me they will make sure the dress is made just as I have sketched it.

I had the ring engraved, too, the same as the Marigny emerald.

Because "Always" is for us, too, Harper. You and I were born two parts of a whole, just as your girls will be. We are Always, and we Always will be.

Like this, I will forever be part of your extraordinary life.

Listen for me on the wind, Harper.

For I will be there, with you,

Always.
Tessa.

THE WORDS SWIM, AND I DROP MY HAND SO MY TEARS WON'T BLUR the ink. Then I lose it completely.

Connor, his own face torn with emotion, pulls me against him in a rough embrace. It is a long time later when he speaks.

"We're lucky, Harper," he says hoarsely. "We're so lucky." I nod against his suit jacket, holding onto it for dear life, until finally I gulp and he pulls away. Brushing a loose curl back into place on the pile atop my head, he smiles wryly. "Careful. If I ruin this, Cass might kill both of us." He wipes his thumbs carefully beneath my eyes and hands me a tissue. I clean up my face.

"Okay?"

"More than okay." He smiles again then turns and puts out his arm. "Shall we?"

~

THE EVENING SKY IS TURNING FROM ROSE TO INDIGO, AND thunder is rumbling in the distance, as Connor's truck approaches the gates leading into our driveway. He turns through them, and I discover that my home has been transformed in my absence.

The live oaks lining the drive are hung with lanterns that turn the Spanish moss to ethereal fantasy. Night jasmine spills from large pottery urns at the bottom of the stairs, and tea lights in filigree cages make dappled patterns on the red magnolia when we park. Connor comes around to open the door for me.

"They're all out back," he says, when I look around at the deserted front porch. He takes my hands to help me down. For a moment we stand there, listening to the distant sound of thunder, the night scented and rich about us, the full moon just rising through the trees. And then he leads me inside.

The makeshift kitchen has been cordoned off behind a delicate Venetian screen, the floorboards leading into the grand reception area polished to a mellow glow. Two lines of standing candelabras, interspersed with indoor plants, make a passage through to the rear salon. Through the open door, I can see twinkling lights among the trees lining the lawn, leading down to my night garden. "It's so beautiful," I whisper.

I had already thought the night garden my own private paradise, but in my absence it has been transformed into Eden itself. A magical oasis of flower-covered benches and candlelight surrounds a circle: made half of the flowers even now opening beneath the night sky and half of the water garden behind it, in which the candles find their reflection. Red magnolia trees are just visible on either edge. The benches face down to the slow-moving, moonlit river. On the jetty stands a wrought iron arch, wended through with the same flowers that once formed my wedding bouquet, and more recently, stood on the table in the dress shop: a wild, unstructured collection of antique rose and amaranthus, dusty miller and dahlias and pink astilbe. The arch feels decadent and dark, as if once I walk through it, I shall never be quite the same. Beyond it, purple storm clouds hover over the river. They're lit from behind by far-off lightning, their deep purple hearts ringed by gold every time the flashes come. Electricity hangs in the air like a force-field, seeming to crackle all around us.

From the salon where I'm standing, the scene is otherworldly. I know with a deep certainty that this night is the beginning of that other world, and the supernatural life I will lead in it. I am suddenly very aware of my brother, and all that he doesn't yet know.

"Are you ready to do this?" Connor says gently, turning to me and taking my hands again.

I press his with my own. "Connor." I suddenly need him to know the truth. "Tonight—our vows—they aren't just for show."

"I guessed as much when Antoine insisted on having a wedding." He smiles wryly. "Your husband isn't really one for meaningless gestures. But in case I was still wondering, he came to see me, to explain his intentions. A little late, perhaps, and not quite the traditional way of asking a man for his sister's hand in marriage. But at least he let me pretend my opinion mattered." His face softens as he sees the tension that must be in mine. "It's okay, Harper. I know that it's the same for you and Antoine as it is for Cass and me. It really is *always*, isn't it?"

"Yes." I hold his eyes, unsure if he understands what I mean. "Always, Connor. Forever. Not . . ." I search for the right words. "Not just until death do us part, but . . . beyond that." I'm not sure what I'm expecting, perhaps for Connor to rear away in horror. But he doesn't. He just turns side-on and offers me his arm once more, his half smile both knowing and amused. "Harper," he murmurs as we move toward the back porch, "I live with a vampire. Do you truly think I don't know the meaning of 'always'?"

Despite the gravity of the moment, laughter bubbles up inside me as we emerge into the soft glow of the lanterns, and that is how the congregation first sees me: my head back, laughing with my brother.

CHAPTER 23

WEDDING

As Connor leads me out onto the porch, I become aware of the pianist to my right and the piece he's playing that is piped all the way down the slope. It is *I Giorni*, by Ludovico Einaudi.

I'm transported back to Antoine on the jetty, the first day we met: *You're listening to Ludovico Einaudi? . . . I Giorni . . .*

Yes. "The Days."

Indeed . . .

Indeed.

I step onto the lawn.

I know there are people watching. I can feel their presence, hear the soft sibilance of their whispers as I approach. But I don't see them.

I'm walking upon land that is my soul, holding my brother's arm, and wearing my sister's love all around me. And ahead, so alive he seems to glimmer in the indigo night, is Antoine. Standing beneath the flowered arch, he seems to be made of both the wild blooms above and the Mississippi storm blazing across the sky behind him.

I pause at the foot of the jetty and smile at my brother. He steps away, seeming to know that from here, I need to go alone. I can hear Tessa whisper on the night breeze, calling me forward. The scent of a river storm is rich and dark on the night, full of power.

The wooden boards feel warm and reassuring beneath the thin sole of my heels. Antoine's eyes go deep cobalt as I approach, darkening as they travel over the moonscape bodice of my gown, the rich garden of silver, indigo, and emerald. I drift across the boards, and it seems to me that the pearl on my right hand glows as I near Antoine, just as the storm seems to intensify in the distance.

"Please," begins the priest, "take your seats." I smile inwardly as I recall the last time I saw him, right after he married Antoine and me the first time. Then the music fades, and there is nothing but the rumble of the distant storm and the thick Mississippi night.

I face Antoine and he takes my hands, his eyes never leaving mine.

"Almost a year ago," says the priest, beaming as he faces the congregation, "a young man came to me with an odd request: that I go to a small church on the outskirts of Natchez. I was to wait there, he said, until a certain hour. If he did not appear before that hour was out, I was to leave and forget that we had ever met. If he came, I was to conduct a wedding." The congregation murmurs with interest, shifting in their seats. I look at Antoine, raising my eyebrows faintly. He gives a slight shrug, his mouth twitching at the corners. "I waited," the priest goes on. "Just as I was about to give the man up as a dreamer, the church door opened—and in came this man and this beautiful young lady."

He makes a slight bow, his arms outstretched to include us both, and a ripple of applause goes through the congregation. "They were young, certainly. But they were certain. They were true. They knew what they meant to do, and they cared nothing for the opinion of others." The congregation sighs collectively. A slightly puzzled look crosses the priest's face. I wonder just how much of that day he genuinely recalls, and how much has been placed there by Antoine. I cast my husband an upward look, and he widens his eyes in a "what, me?" expression of innocence that does absolutely nothing to dispel my suspicions.

"However, their vows, though beautifully done, are not the thing I recollect most of that day." I can't help but wonder where he is headed with this. "It was late summer," says the priest. "When I entered the church to wait for the young couple, there was a magnolia tree by the door. I remember looking at it and thinking that it was sad the summer was all but gone, and the magnolias with it." My heart skips a beat in surprise. I hadn't expected this. "Barely an hour later," the priest goes on, "after Antoine and Harper Marigny had exchanged their vows, I followed them out into the sunlight." He shakes his head slowly, wonder creasing his face. "Imagine my astonishment, when I saw that same tree had burst into new flower. Red magnolias bloomed on every branch. They littered the ground and scented the breeze. I knew then that I had married no ordinary couple. I knew their union was a miracle, blessed by God himself."

Lightning from afar flashes behind purple cloud, and Antoine and I stare at one another. I know that memory isn't one Antoine placed in the priest's head. I can see in his face that Antoine is as thunderstruck as I am. The priest may have been compelled first to forget us, and then to remember. But this memory is not compelled or created. This memory is what he saw, what he knew in his heart, and somehow, that is a gift almost more magical than any memory I hold of that day.

"Love is always a miracle. I consider myself blessed to witness this miracle not once, but twice." The priest smiles at me, and there is such love in his eyes I feel as if there is a force beyond us all that speaks through him when he says, "Ladies and gentlemen, we are gathered here today, to celebrate the union of this man, and this woman."

From there, his words cease to matter and simply wash over me. I don't see him. I see only Antoine in front of me, his eyes the cobalt of the distant thunderheads and lit, just as they are, by brilliant gold flashes as he stares at me. I'm dimly aware of us both reciting the vows, but somehow it seems that all we need to say has already been said, contained in the priest's memory and kind words. Tate steps forward, and I realize with a shock that he must have been there the whole time. His smile as he holds out the rings is so filled with emotion that it touches my soul. It was worth getting married all over again, I think, just to see that look on Tate's face. His presence at Antoine's side is something I doubt either of them could ever have imagined during the long years in which they were estranged. It's a reminder that it is not only Antoine and I who have traveled a long road to get here. Immortality, I think, creates bonds unimaginable in a human lifespan. And soon, I too will be immortal. Suddenly I want that promise of forever with a fierce, deep longing.

I slide the silver band onto Antoine's finger and hold my own out for him to place the emerald back upon it. I feel the comforting weight slip over my knuckle and know, deep in my soul, that I will never be without it again.

Always.

"Mr. Marigny." The priest smiles at Antoine. "You may kiss your bride."

A clap of thunder cracks the air, so loudly the congregation shrieks, closely followed by a gust of wind so powerful the women clutch their hats, and the arch above us shivers. "Tessa," I whisper, smiling, and it is then Antoine catches my mouth with his own.

"Abatey," he murmurs against it.

"Vampire," I murmur back.

His lips smile on mine. Then I know nothing except his kiss and the promise it holds, in this life—and the next.

~

DESPITE THE CRACKLING OVER THE RIVER, THE STORM HOLDS OFF as waiters move among us with champagne and finger food, which take the place of a traditional dinner, to my relief. I would have found a sit-down formal dinner unbearable.

My Deepwater Hollow school friends are full of breathless congratulations that I suspect have more to do with the huge, silver ice buckets full of Veuve than any deep emotion, though they mean well enough. I'm more interested in the guest I don't know: a rangy, lean young man with long, shaggy hair, a vicious scar across his throat, and eyes far older than his face. He stands on the edge of the party, distinctly apart. I can feel him watching me as we move along the congratulatory crowd until we reach him. I think for a moment that he has stepped forward, until I realize that for some reason, it is the people around him who have stepped back, leaving him alone. He addresses Antoine directly.

"Well, Marigny. A miracle indeed, I believe." He casts Antoine a sardonic smile that strikes me, once again, as being at odds with his youthful face. "Madame Marigny," he says, inclining his head in a curiously graceful, old-world manner that is almost a bow. "I cannot tell you how glad I am to meet you."

"Thank you." I smile at him as he takes my hand, trying not to shy away from the intense scrutiny in his gray eyes. "I'm so sorry, I don't think I got your name."

"No. You didn't." He flashes me a grin that can only be described as wolfish, and suddenly I know why the humans behind me have taken a wary step backward. "Monsieur le Comte de Ainhoa, Madame, *à votre service.*" He bows again, then winks at me and shrugs with an insoucience that is uncannily like Remy's. "But we are in America, where such titles don't matter; and my friends call me Guidry." My surprise must be palpable, for he murmurs, "I age well, do I not?" He flashes me a wry, slightly twisted grin before turning back to Antoine. "Your husband won the right to call me friend long ago," he adds as I make an effort to recover my composure. "And more recently, he won it a second time." Guidry nods behind him, where Remy and his pack lounge uneasily even further from the edges of the party. I'm touched they're here, knowing how uncomfortable they feel on Marigny ground. Vampire ground.

Antoine lifts his eyebrows as he follows Guidry's glance. "Remy is your kin?"

"Sure, the man is kin." Guidry gives Antoine a quizzical look. "You didn't know?"

Antoine shakes his head wonderingly. "No. I did not." He gives a soft cough of laughter. "But that figures, Guidry. It does, indeed." He puts his hand out, and the young man grasps it strongly. Though he isn't young, I remind myself. He may look barely older than Jeremiah, but if what I recall is correct, he's known Antoine for almost three centuries.

"I'm grateful to you, Marigny." Guidry glances across at Remy and back at Antoine. "For the second time in my life, it seems I'm in your debt. Doubly so, since you transformed my kin as you once did me."

"Your debt to me was long discharged, Guidry, as your kin has already discharged theirs." Antoine grasps the hand before him firmly. "I'm glad you came, old friend."

Guidry snorts under his breath. "Look around you, Marigny. This night is a gathering the likes of which has never been seen before and will likely not be seen again. Vampires, wolves, and the gods alone know what else, if what I hear is true." He nods at me. "You have taken unto yourself a bride of particular quality, old friend. And there is not one here who would not willingly die to see her safe." Drawing Antoine close, he murmurs just loud enough for me to hear, "And I bring word from others of your kind, some old friends, others you don't know. They say they will see your young born safe, and fight if they are called upon. You are not alone, Marigny. Remember that."

"Guidry is right." As Tate materializes at our side, Guidry instantly backs away, all trace of amiability gone.

"You," he says curtly.

"Yes, Guidry. Me."

The two men stare at each other for a long, charged moment during which I begin to wonder if swords might make a modern reappearance. Then Tate smiles. He raises his glass to Antoine, his face curiously animated. "You are not alone, Antoine. And Guidry is right in saying we would all die to ensure your family's safety. Though you will allow me to hope it doesn't come to that."

Guidry makes a dismissive noise. "If it does, you can be grateful that the wolves are here, Takatoka."

"Oh," says Tate lightly. "I am grateful, cousin."

"Cousin?" I look between them curiously. "The two of you are related?"

"By marriage only," snaps Guidry. He glares at Tate. "Let's just say that in modern terminology, my people came from the wrong side of the Natchez tracks. Or river, as the case might be."

Antoine steps in between them. "And more than two centuries lie between us and old quarrels. Perhaps the two of you can draw blood another time."

"Ha." Guidry snorts, but he subsides and wanders off to join the wolves. Tate swallows his wine and turns to talk to one of the teachers.

"I guess it wouldn't be a wedding without family arguments," Antoine murmurs, raising his eyebrows. Around us the music has picked up, and people have begun dancing. Antoine draws me close and we begin to move together.

"He's so young." I shake my head, bewildered. "It's odd, seeing such old eyes look out from such a youthful face."

"Guidry was barely twenty-one when he became what he is," Antoine says.

"You activated him," I say, frowning. "Why didn't I know that?"

He shrugs. "It didn't seem important."

"Is that the other reason you invited him? Because of that bond?"

"No. Guidry is my friend. One of my only ones, if I'm honest." His smile is almost as wolfish as his friend's. "But I confess, I'm happy with anything that will keep you safe, Mrs. Marigny."

"Shouldn't that be *Madame?*"

Antoine rolls his eyes. "In the days in which that title could have been applied, you, my darling wife, would have been shunned as a shameless hussy."

"I rather like the idea of being a shameless hussy."

"Well," he growls in a low voice that makes my blood run thick and hot through my veins, "give me enough time to play nice with our guests, and I'll take you upstairs and turn you into one."

"Give me enough time to play nice," I murmur back, "and I'll take you upstairs and seduce you like one." His chuckle sends a quiver down my spine. He spins me in a twirl, and as I come back into his embrace, Remy is standing to one side, unsmiling.

"Remy." We come to an abrupt halt. "What is it? Is it Keziah?"

"No." Remy's hard expression suddenly cracks. "Have you seen Avery?"

"Oh, Remy." I reach for him but he pulls away, his mouth grim and tight. "No," I say quietly. "I haven't seen Avery since I left Cass's house. She should be here somewhere, though." He nods briefly and pushes away through the crowd, barely acknowledging Connor and Cass, who are dancing nearby. From the corner of my eye, I see Callie watching him through narrowed eyes. She's standing by the bar, next to Jeremiah, who, if appearance is anything to go, by, has already drunk way too much. He looks sad, and I suspect Remy is not the only person wondering where Avery has gone. Callie, still watching Remy, glances back at Jeremiah and says something. He shrugs, turning back to his drink. Callie's face hardens. Seeming to weigh the odds, she turns and crosses the lawn. She takes Remy by the elbow and murmurs something in his ear. Remy rears back and looks at her in surprise, then takes her by the arms, as if he's asking her something urgent. A moment later he is gone, streaking at preternatural speed through the night.

"What did you do?" I ask Callie as she comes back down the lawn.

"I told Remy where to find Avery." The look she gives me is slightly belligerent, as if she's expecting me to challenge her.

"And where is that?"

"In the library, of course." Callie rolls her eyes impatiently. "From what Jeremiah has told me, the library was where Connor broke Avery's heart back in the day. And it's the place Keziah first found her. Avery ran off not long after the ceremony was finished. Right about when she saw Remy and the pack among the guests."

"And you know she went to the library how, exactly?"

"Because it's what we do, isn't it?" Callie looks sideways at me. "We go back to the places that mean the most to us. The library is where Avery was broken. Makes sense it's where she goes to try to understand herself." She colors slightly. "Also, I followed her. She's in a mood. I was worried Jeremiah might notice and go after her."

"So you sent Remy to her instead?" I look at her skeptically. "Are you certain Remy's the right person for Avery right now?"

"Of course he is." Callie shakes her head. "For someone who seems so wise all the time, you can be seriously thick, Harper. Remy loves Avery. Avery loves him." She gives me a slightly evil grin. "And frankly, if I have to use your wedding to make them both see that before Avery sets off to college with Jeremiah, then I'm *so* going to do it."

She backs off as Antoine comes closer, shooting me a final, less-than-honorable grin.

"We need to move everyone inside," Antoine murmurs in my ear. "Apparently, we're not allowed to leave until after we've cut the cake."

"I thought we had to do speeches?"

"We can make that quick."

"I thought this wedding was your idea. Didn't you want to do it properly?"

"Sure." His grin is just as evil as Callie's was and more. "But there's a storm coming, and I don't see any reason we can't do it quickly."

I'm laughing, but my eyes are on Guidry, standing on the edge of the lawn, watching us through dark eyes. I look up at Antoine. "Can you hold off just a little? I want to speak with your friend a moment."

"Guidry?" Antoine's brow creases. "You trying to learn my secrets?"

I laugh. "Something like that, yes. I won't be long." I touch his cheek and move through the crowd. It's unsettling being the center of attention. I keep forgetting the party is mine and expecting to fade into the background. I find myself looking forward to the moment Antoine and I can escape. "Guidry." I'm aware he's been watching me approach.

"Madame Marigny." He does the slight head-bow thing again, and I can't help but feel as if I'm a guest at an eighteenth-century ball rather than a twenty-first-century wedding.

"I have a question," I say. "It's rather personal, but I have my own reasons for asking it."

"Ah." He raises his eyebrows and takes a large swallow of whiskey. "What is it that you want to know about your husband? I can't promise to tell you. Some secrets are best left in the past." He smiles wickedly.

"Nothing like that," I say hastily. "It isn't about Antoine himself." I pause, wondering how exactly to broach the question. "It's about how you were . . . activated." He doesn't answer, just watches me quietly. "I'm not asking about the process, or the circumstances in which it happened. Both are between you and Antoine." I don't look away from him. "I'm asking because you're still alive, more than two centuries after you became a wolf."

"And you want to know if that's normal," he says. "Because your brother is a wolf."

I nod.

He looks at me quizzically. "You mean Antoine doesn't know?"

"Antoine said you used to be a wolf, but that he doesn't know what you are now."

"I am what Antoine made me." Guidry's voice is low, meant only for me, his eyes holding mine. "I've met other wolves during my life. They were larger than most men and lived longer, usually staying healthy and active well into their nineties. But they did age, and they did die." One large hand gestures briefly to his own face. "I haven't aged. And I've outlived them all."

I inhale sharply. A hard smile lifts the corners of his mouth. "Tell your brother he will live as long as that vampire he seems so bound to—so long as she doesn't bite him, of course. Even an immortal wolf can't survive vampire venom. I was bitten once, and it took all the wisdom of an extremely powerful witch to save me. Vampires are the one thing that actually can kill us."

His eyes shift across the lawn to where Antoine is politely dancing with Miss Calhoun, who is staring up at him with something akin to awe. "And tell your husband," Guidry says dryly, "that I should be insulted he thought me something other than the wolf he made." He casts me a grin that takes the sting out of his words and slips away, into the shadows where the pack are drinking together. I'm guessing they, too, are unaware of what Antoine's blood means for their mortality.

The song ends, and Antoine bows gallantly over Miss Calhoun's hand. A moment later, he is at my side. "If you're done," he says, eyes glittering, "can we do those speeches now?"

I open my mouth to tell him what I've learned, but then I close it again. There'll be time for that. And there's someone else I need to talk to first.

CHAPTER 24

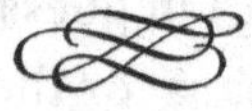

STORM

$\mathcal{A}$very and Remy appear a moment later. Remy has Avery's hand fast in his own, and something of his old insouciance is back in his eyes. Avery's face is flushed and tearstained, but her smile is so bright it outshines the lightning flashing over the sky. "We've been sent to kidnap you," she says, taking my hand. "Tate is bringing everyone inside," she explains as she leads us around the side of the mansion, pulling slightly ahead of Remy and Antoine.

"Happy?" I whisper, as we enter the mansion through the front steps I'd come in only a couple of hours earlier.

"Oh, Harper." She grips my hand and pulls me close against her, putting her head briefly on my shoulder. "It turns out he was just as miserable as me. And I don't care what my parents think. I don't care that we might never have children." She smiles up at me and kisses my cheek. "The only thing I care about is that he actually loves me."

I hug her. "I'm so glad, Avery."

We wait in the quiet kitchen as Tate, on the back porch, taps his glass and calls the crowd to come inside. Avery fiddles with my hair and dress, then she and Remy disappear to join the others. Antoine nods over my shoulder. "There's one person who wants to see you before the speeches."

I turn to find Iara in the shadows beneath the staircase, breathtakingly beautiful in scarlet silk with a matching flower deep in the pile of dark curls on her head. "I have to come," she says, her English more broken than usual. "I will hide, yes, but I have to see you. To tell you *felicidades*—congratulations." She takes my hands with such genuine warmth I am touched to my soul. "I am so happy, Harper. For you, and your *bebes*. This night, she is so, beautiful, no? Is perfect." Her smile is tremulous. "I want to say, thankyou. For giving me a new family. A new home." She squeezes my hands. "And now, you go, and have your speeches, yes?"

I press my cheek to hers, my heart warm with love. "Thankyou," I whisper in her ear. "Thankyou for helping me get back to my sister."

Antoine waits until Iara steps away, then holds out his arm to me. "Ready?"

I nod, slipping my arm through his, catching my breath as he bends to touch his lips to mine. "Ready."

We stand at the entrance to the rear salon, which is ablaze with candelabra. Low couches are arrayed against the walls. In the center is a tall creation wended with the same flowers from my arch, standing on a lone circular table.

"Ladies and gentlemen," Tate begins, as everyone turns to look at us. "May I present Mr. and Mrs. Antoine Marigny."

The crowd raises their glasses, a sea of faces toasting our future. I try to make sense of what everyone says after that, but I find it difficult to think at all.

I'm officially, publicly, Harper Marigny now.

Forever.

~

THE SOUND OF APPLAUSE IS STILL RESOUNDING IN MY EARS AS Antoine goes to lead me from the salon.

"Antoine!" I'm laughing, breathless. "Everyone is still here."

"And there's plenty of booze to keep them happy. We've already said our formal goodbyes. Come. I want to take that dress off with my teeth." He raises his eyebrows. "Unless you want to stay . . .?"

"Definitely not," I say fervently. Crowds and I don't mix well. "Wait." I pause on the bottom step. "There's something I have to do first."

He looks down at me, eyes glittering. "Does it have to be now?"

Somewhere close by, I hear the low rumble of Remy's voice. "Yes." I touch his arm. "It does. I need to find my brother." I touch his arm as I turn, heading back through the crowd, smiling and nodding as I make my way to the front porch where Connor, his tie loose and shirt open at the neck, is rolling a glass of whiskey in his hand. He's leaning against one of the columns and Cass is leaning against him. It is so like my brother, I think, to be out here in the quiet, while a full-blown party takes place behind him.

We are alike, that way.

"Connor."

He turns around in surprise, drawing Cass with him. "Harper. I thought you'd left." His mouth curls. "Antoine didn't really seem in the mood to linger."

I shake my head, smiling. "There's something I thought you should know first." I look between him and Cass. "I learned something tonight. I wanted you to be the first to know."

"More surprises, Harper?" Connor's still smiling, but his eyes are wary. I don't blame him. Lately, most of my surprises have been volcanic. Cass, too, looks tense. I smile, trying to reassure them both.

"It's about Guidry. Antoine's old friend."

"The wolf." Connor's smile fades entirely. "What new disaster has he brought news of?" Connor pulls Cass tightly to his side, as if bracing them both for whatever is coming.

"No, Connor. Not a disaster at all." I go on hastily before he becomes more alarmed. "I wanted you to know that it was Antoine who activated Guidry." I wait, but when there's no glimmer of comprehension in Connor's face, I go on. "More than two centuries ago, Connor. Guidry is almost as old as Antoine himself."

"Wait." Cass steps forward, hope and fear warring in her eyes. She clutches my arm, hard enough to leave marks. I force myself not to flinch. "You mean, there's no other magic involved? That Guidry has lived this long because it was Antoine who activated him?"

"That's exactly what I mean." I look between them, my heart almost hurting at the slowly dawning hope on my brother's face.

"You're sure," Connor says roughly.

"As sure as we can be." I nod. "Guidry has met other wolves over the years. None have lived so long, and they've all aged, if more slowly than humans. But Guidry himself has never aged at all. He's unchanged from the day he was made."

Connor is staring at me, eyes like burning coals in his face. "How is it that Antoine never knew this?"

"I don't know." I lift my shoulders slightly. "I haven't told him yet."

Connor steps forward, his eyes holding mine. "You came to tell me this before you told Antoine?"

"I thought you should be the first to know." My eyes shift to Cass. "That you should both be the first to know."

"Oh, Harper." Cass's hand flies to her mouth, tears filling her eyes. A moment later Connor has caught me in a hard embrace, his arms crushing me against him, his heart tripping wildly under my cheek.

"Thank you," my brother murmurs against my head. "Thank you so much."

~

A LONG TIME LATER I SLIP INSIDE, TO FIND ANTOINE WAITING AT the bottom of the stairs. "Now," he says dryly, "can we finally go upstairs?"

I pause as sounds come from the library. I wrap my arms around his neck. "Can you hear that?"

"What?" Antoine rolls his eyes. "Someone is having fun. Let's not be too curious, Harper."

"Not just someone." I smile. "Listen." A moment later, a familiar chuckle rumbles through the mansion, followed by a low growl of amusement, then animated conversation. Antoine's eyebrows rise.

"Well. It sounds like Guidry and Remy are hitting it off."

I nod. "I imagine they've got a lot to talk about."

He casts me a curious look. "And why is that?"

"You have no idea why Guidry is so grateful to you, do you?"

"Guidry saved my life many times over the years." Antoine shrugs dismissively. "Whatever my blood gave him he has given back, just like I said. And," he says, his voice lowering as his mouth grazes my throat, "we've better things to do than talk about Guidry."

"Antoine, wait." I lean back inside his embrace so I can meet his eyes. "You said earlier that you didn't know what Guidry had become. I think you meant that he must have found some magic that kept him from aging."

Antoine frowns, but doesn't answer.

"He didn't find other magic, Antoine." I hold his eyes. "Your blood was the magic. Guidry has met others of his kind. They all aged and died eventually—but he never has."

Awareness flares in Antoine's eyes, comprehension

spreading slowly across his face. "Then you mean that Remy, the pack . . . Connor . . . ?" His voice breaks off as I nod.

"Yes," I say. "All of them, according to Guidry. If they have your blood, they're here to stay, just like you or Tate." I smile at his astonishment. "Guidry thought you knew. He said to tell you he's rather insulted that you thought he was *something other than what you made him*." That makes Antoine laugh, though I can see in his eyes that it will take a while for the information to truly sink in. From the library, I hear Avery's voice, excited and happy.

"I'm so glad they're back together."

"Really." Antoine sweeps me up before I have time to protest, holding me against his chest as he turns for the stairs. "To be honest, I've given them next to no thought at all."

"You don't mean that," I protest as he kicks my door open.

"Don't I," he growls, carrying me over to the bed.

"But surely you're happy for them? They've been so miserable, apart."

"I couldn't"—he lowers me to the bed—"be happier." I can't help laughing at that. Running his hand down the bodice of my dress, he makes a low sound in his throat that turns my laugh into a quite different sound. "This dress," he says, "is like your garden under a full moon."

"You see that," I breathe.

"Of course I see that." He pulls the pins from my hair, spreading it with his hands. "I've never seen anything more beautiful in my life than you walking toward me, wearing it."

Part of me is astonished that he should see so instantly what I do in the dress, but another part of me is entirely unsurprised. *That is what's between us,* I think. A knowing that transcends life. A place where we both seem to understand the other before conscious thought. I stroke his face. "You know that Tessa designed it?"

He nods. "Connor told me. And I saw the box it came in." He

nods to the corner, where all the things of mine that had been at Cass's are in a neat stack. Among them is the large white dress box, with a name in curlicued writing embossed on the lid: *Maison de Lysette.*

"An old friend of yours?" I try to make my voice neutral, but something in it must alert him, because Antoine grins.

"Not that kind of friend." He strokes a thumb over my neck, making me shiver. "Although I admit, when I knew her, Madame Lysette ran a boutique of a rather different kind."

My eyes widen. "As in . . .?"

He chuckles. "There's a reason she goes by the name *Madame Lysette.* Several racy eighteenth-century memoirs feature her establishment in—shall we say, rather lurid detail."

"Wow."

"Indeed."

We're both laughing, and then his face sobers once more. "That priest," he says, his hand splayed over my waist. "I didn't tell him to say what he did. About the magnolia tree."

"I know that." I reach up and cup his face, feeling the faint roughness of stubble under my palm. "He genuinely recalled it, I think."

"He said our marriage was blessed by God." Antoine's mouth is trailing down my neck.

"But we both know those flowers were because of the Abatey inside me," I gasp, arching up toward his mouth.

"Do we?" He pulls back from me, stroking my face with his hand. "We don't know what it is that makes this magic possible," he says, his touch making me shiver. "For all we think we know, the reality is that too much of what I am—and what you are—is unknown. That priest shouldn't have remembered anything of that day other than what I commanded him to recall. But instead, he remembered that tree. The way it flowered. For some reason, he knew something he shouldn't have, and it touched him emotionally, to the point where even compulsion didn't eliminate it. What is that, Harper, if not magic?"

He holds my face as I shake my head slowly. "I don't know, Antoine," I whisper. "I don't understand any of it."

"How could you?" Lightning beyond the window lights the half smile on his face. The storm is coming closer. "How can any of us understand what is happening here? You hold within your veins the power of water. I am immortal, but my blood can activate power in others. And somehow you're pregnant with my children, Harper. With twins who can time travel. How is any of that rational?" He kisses me as thunder rumbles over the lawn. "I choose to believe the priest remembered that tree on his own," he says, his lips moving against my cheek, "because he felt something that day. Something beyond what I compelled him to know, or to forget. I choose to believe that whatever was strong enough to bind you to me that day, it had an effect on him, just as it did on the tree next to the church. And if that is true—then, Harper, we have a magic all of our own. And after all this time, all we have been through, I want to believe that. I *need* to believe that."

"Me, too." I rise up off the bed and kiss him, drinking him into my soul. "And soon there will be new magic in our lives, Antoine. Magic beyond anything we know now. And I promise you this." As thunder claps and lightning lights the night beyond, I hold him close. "I promise that I will be beside you to keep our daughters safe. I promise. Do you hear me?" The thunder rattles the walls of the mansion, breaking so loudly I have to yell above it, the lightning showing his face in stark relief. "I will be here!" I hold his face in my hands. "Always, Antoine. I swear it."

Antoine sweeps me from the bed. Carrying me to the wide French windows, he places me down on the sill so the wind rips through my dress, making me laugh exultantly. He places his hands on my belly, his eyes lit by the raging storm. "I will never let you go," he says roughly. "Not now, Harper. Not ever. We are in this life together. Always."

The clouds break, and rain tumbles down in a river that drenches the ground below us in seconds, dousing candles and sending trestle tables flying. On the jetty, the wrought iron arch remains, the flowers wound through it rippling in the wild wind as if they are being seduced by it. The wind carries dusky petals of dahlia through the window to land, soft and fragrant, on the bare floorboards. Below us, our guests are shrieking with laughter, taking shelter on the porch, spilling out both ends of the mansion, their excited chatter whisked away on the wind and drumming rain coming off the roof in sheets. Wild calls cut the night, and through the window I see the pack, still in human form, running through the rain down toward the river, white shirts plastered to their skin. My brother is running with them. As they reach the water, they leap into the air, shifting into their animal forms as they disappear into the shadows. A moment later savage, thrilling yowls join the sounds of the storm, and I shiver with delight at the wolves' triumphant calls. Cass, her dress clinging to her lean body, pauses by the river. Turning toward the mansion, she raises one arm in a silent salute, as if she knows I'm watching. Then she disappears, following the wolves into the night.

Thunder cracks about us and rain runs in rivulets down my neck, into my dress. I pull Antoine down to meet me and he takes my lips, bruisingly hard.

"Always," I murmur against him. "Always and forever, Antoine."

EPILOGUE

$\mathcal{D}$ear Tessa,

It is the early hours of the morning, and the storm is still at last.

I will have more to write, soon. A whole world to tell you of, I'm sure.

But for now I want you to know this.

I felt your touch in my dress. I heard your whisper on the wind. Even if Connor hadn't given me your letter, I would have known you were there.

The way ahead is unknown, Tessa. It is dark, and full of magic I cannot see.

But the greatest magic of all is knowing that you are here, that you always will be. That no matter what this life brings, you will be a part of it, forever.

Tonight, the moon gleams down upon my water garden, still covered in dahlias fallen from my wedding arch. In the centre of the pond rise two tall green shoots, their buds yet still tightly furled, protecting the twin secrets within.

My babies.

When they come, my human life will be over, and my immortal one will begin.

I am glad you will be with me, Tessa.

Always.

Your twin,
Harper.

BLUE LILIES SAMPLE

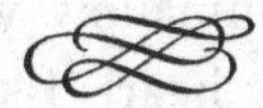

PROLOGUE

ear Tessa,

FALL CAME AND WENT, THEN WINTER. NOW THE FIRST SHOOTS OF spring are poking through the earth. I feel as if the time has passed in a haze. In just a few weeks, Antoine and I will meet our twins in person. It still doesn't feel real. Sometimes I stand in front of the mirror staring at my belly, thinking of everything that led me to here. But reality isn't like that, is it? We don't carry all that has gone before with us, into every new day. We can only live one day, one moment, one experience, at a time. So no matter all that has gone before, when I look at my belly now, all I know is that I'm pregnant with twin girls I can't wait to meet. That I'm in love with my husband more than I ever imagined possible. And that my world feels full of love, and hope.

I do try to remind myself of the other side of that reality. That my twin girls are time travelers, for example, with powers none of us understand yet. Or the fact that my husband is a vampire. The fact that Keziah, an ancient and dangerous enemy, is lurking unseen somewhere in our world, lying in wait for the birth of our twins so she can take them for her own. Or that the only way I can be sure to keep myself and our girls safe from Keziah is to become a vampire myself, the moment after they are born.

My sensible mind knows all those things. Somehow, though, pregnancy has put a marshmallow wall between my sensible mind and the world of my heart. I spend pretty much all my time on the heart side of the wall, blissfully ignoring the sensible arguments.

When I do allow myself to think of the time after the twins are born, I want to seize every day that I have left in my human body. That isn't hard. Being pregnant with twins is more than enough to keep me firmly focused on my physical body. I am so huge Antoine insists on carrying me down the stairs every time he catches me trying to take them on foot, and weeding my garden is a long-distant memory. I can barely see my feet, let alone what is growing underneath them. At this point, the thought of having an unchanging body that doesn't feel pain is like a fantasy. So I guess you could say that while I'm definitely focused on my human body, right now I'm not feeling any sadness at all about trading it in for a more resilient model.

I can only make jokes like that in these letters to you, since everyone else seems to find them upsetting. Antoine evades any real discussion about my becoming a vampire. We're in agreement it has to happen. But I know that even if he understands it is the smartest course, part of him hates the thought of what I may become.

I don't believe the magic that runs through my veins will become a dark force, as Caleb's did. Antoine's blood, and the medicine woman that lives in it, activated the natural magic in mine in a way Caleb's never was. If we are right, Keziah killed Caleb before he was fully activated. Nor was he an Abatey, the living embodiment of a water spirit. But even if I feel certain I will not become what Caleb was, I'd be lying if I said I'm not afraid of what will happen. The truth is that nobody really knows what I will be after I become a vampire.

There is a lot we don't know.

Tate and Iara went away soon after our wedding. Iara isn't safe here, and Tate wanted her help to discover what he can about Taíno and Warao history. At least, that's what he told us. By the way he was looking at Iara when they left, I suspect there's more to him wanting her by his side than he is admitting, even to himself.

Tate thinks the local stories in Haiti and down in Venezuela might tell us more about Keziah. The wolves, too, have their own legends, so Remy and Connor are working together to find what they can. Since the arrival of Guidry, Antoine's old friend and Remy's distant ancestor, all trace of animosity between them seems gone. The knowledge Guidry brought—that Antoine's blood not only made them wolf but also imparted the gift of immortality—has been both liberating and, I suspect, daunting. While the knowledge seems to have set Connor free, allowing him to finally see a true future with Cass, I suspect it has thrown up new challenges for the pack.

Despite the shock of adjusting to an eternity as a wolf, Remy remains devoted to Avery, who is away at college. Remy's sudden willingness to help research Keziah is due more, I think, to a desire to remain linked to Avery than anything else. By the way Remy looks every time Avery's name is mentioned, and the amount of time he spends talking to her on the phone, distance isn't a barrier to their rekindled relationship.

Callie has already been accepted into Old Miss to study pre-med. I'm going to miss her terribly when she goes away to college. By then, the twins will have been born.

And that brings me back to where I started.

The reality, both in my heart and my mind, is that I can't even begin to imagine what life will look like after our girls are born. I don't know what I will be, or even what, exactly, they will be. I try to think of everything you told me, Tessa. That the twins visited you all your life. That you saw them grown into young women. That they helped bring my wedding dress to life. I tell myself that all those things mean I have nothing to worry about.

But another, fearful part of me wonders if all those memories belong to one of the water paths Iara spoke about. If something happens to harm the twins, during the birth or after, will I simply find myself on another water path? Will it be as if they never existed at all? Worst of all, will I be the only one able to remember everything that's happened?

As fantastic as they might seem, these are the thoughts that haunt me and can send me spiraling into terror.

The water lilies that showed just above the water when I first discovered my pregnancy still have yet to unfurl. Over winter the color of the buds changed, so that the glimpse of the petals beneath now shows as a deep indigo. They look more like an Egyptian lotus than they do a lily. I've never seen their like grow here. To be honest, I'm not certain I've ever seen anything like them.

But they have yet to flower, Tessa. They should have unfurled long ago, and yet they remain tightly closed, barely showing above the surface of the pond. I check them every morning to make sure they are still there. And every day when I find them still alive, I realize I've been holding my breath, terrified that I will find that they've simply disappeared.

I know this is a long letter. I've been writing to you much more often since the wedding. I guess I know, now, that you're truly here with us. I don't have to wonder if you're listening. I know you are. Every bird call, every whisper of breeze, carries part of you on it. I may no longer be able to touch you, Tessa, or ever see you again. But I know you're with me, and that is the greatest comfort I have.

Outside the air is hushed. Spring might be here, but our garden is still, and waiting, as we all are.

Inside, the twins are moving restlessly.

It won't be long, now, until all our questions are answered... one way or another.

Your twin,

Harper

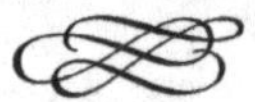

CHAPTER 1

It's early morning, and a slow mist rises over the river. I'm sitting with my bare feet in the cool water of the pond in my night garden, staring at the unopened water lilies, as if I can will them to unfurl simply by looking at them. The garden around me is silent and still. Moisture dripping from the trees is the only sound in the dawn hush. I woke an hour ago, when it was still dark, to find Antoine gone. He's been hunting more often than he used to. Although he hasn't said so, I'm certain he's building his strength ahead of the twins' birth. We both know that he's going to need it.

I try to lift my feet out of the water and stand up, but I'm so big now that even the simplest of movements is like a comedy of errors. Finally I roll over onto my hands and knees, only to find myself staring at a pair of very long, denim-clad legs.

"Can I help at all?" The humor in Antoine's voice is unmistakable. He's standing with his hands thrust into the back pockets of his jeans, his shirt open at the neck and his hair still wet from the shower. He looks like he could have stepped off the cover of a magazine, but his face seems to wear a perpetual frown lately, and even well-fed and rested, he looks drawn, unlike his usual self. We're both scared of what is coming, just as much as we're excited to finally meet our daughters.

"I feel like you're enjoying this just a little too much," I grumble. He gathers me up as easily as if I were a child, rather than the size of a baby elephant, and sets me gently on my feet, his hands still resting loosely on what used to be my hips. He's smiling, the early morning sun picking out the gold in his eyes from the fathomless cobalt behind them, his skin seeming to radiate the rays themselves in a bronze glow. He's impossibly beautiful, and impossible not to love.

"There are a thousand inappropriate jokes I could make about you being on your knees, but by the look on your face, I'm guessing none of them would be wise just now." His voice is low and rich and still makes my stomach turn over.

"Excellent guess."

"Tate called." Antoine picks a leaf out of my hair. "He and Iara are coming back. They should be here in the next few days."

"Good?" I don't know if it is or not. Keziah can sense Iara's presence, just as she can Cass's and Antoine's. The statue Tessa gave me for Iara seems to be a kind of shield, even though Iara can still hear Keziah calling her. We had wondered, when Tate and Iara went to South America, if Keziah would know. We never found out. Keziah disappeared after Cass told her we had bound Iara in the cellar beneath the mansion. Iara remained out of sight after that, until she and Tate went away. Whether Keziah believed Cass or not is a mystery. I doubt she's been wasting the months of my pregnancy, though. Keziah will be back. It's only a question of when.

"Tate said he and Iara are bringing someone back here with them. He wanted to warn me, given how close we are to the twins being born." Antoine seems calm enough. "It's a shaman from Iara's tribe. He offered to come, apparently. Tate thinks he can help protect you during the birth."

"That's a good thing?" Again, I'm not sure.

"I guess so." Antoine looks as unconvinced as I feel. "We'll find out when we meet him."

"A shaman." I say it doubtfully. Sometimes I feel as if we're magnets, drawing every kind of supernatural to us. Equally, if it can help keep our babies safe, I will take any kind of supernatural there is.

"We'll have a full house, soon enough," I say. "Callie mentioned Jeremiah was talking about coming back for spring break, too." Since Jeremiah went away to college last fall, the riverside house he and Antoine had once shared has been more or less closed up. Antoine still keeps some things there, more so that Jeremiah will know he has a home of his own than for any other reason, I suspect. At Christmas, though, Jeremiah had come straight to the mansion and stayed for the duration. I expect he'll do the same this time. He likes to be close to Antoine, and my due date is right on top of spring break.

"It will be good to see him." Antoine gives me a smile that doesn't quite relax the tension in his eyes. "I'm sure it will be fine." It's not clear if he's talking about the Warao shaman, the full house we'll have, the birth, or my becoming a vampire.

Take your pick. I return his smile with one I'm sure he finds just as unconvincing as I do his. "Of course it will."

His eyes move from my face to the pond behind me, and his smile fades, taking with it the gold from his eyes. "Please tell me you weren't sitting with your feet in that pond."

"I'm not going to suddenly time travel every time I'm in water, Antoine. It would make showering difficult, don't you think?"

"That pond isn't just any water, and you know it." He's unamused by my attempt at levity. "Everything about your garden is filled with magic. It also just happens to be the place Keziah found you last time." His eyes lock onto mine, and although his voice is gentle, all trace of humor is gone. "I think it's time we started being very careful, Harper. We're less than two weeks away from your due date. Keziah will know that as well as we do. She won't be far away."

Despite the mild temperature, I can't suppress a shiver. "Surely we would know if she had come back? The wolves always know if she's nearby. Guidry said there are others of your kind who can help us, if we call on them." Guidry originally came from the same bayous as Remy's pack, though he predates the existing wolves by more than two centuries.

"Yes, we have the alliance with Guidry and the pack. And the European vampires he knows have offered their help, it's true. But all the reinforcements in the world can't protect us against Keziah if she finds a way of getting to you or the twins, Harper. We can't let that happen."

"I know." I put my hands on his face. "But I'm not going into labor today, Antoine. And she won't dare take me before they're born. She'll be too afraid something might go wrong. Keziah wants our girls alive and well." I swallow my distaste. Antoine's own face has turned to stone. "I know how hard it is for us to talk about this," I say quietly. "But at some point, we need to talk about how you're going to turn me, Antoine."

I could also mention the mysterious vampire friends of Guidry's whom Antoine never brings up, but who seem to know an awful lot about us—or Guidry himself, whom I've barely met, though he's one of Antoine's oldest friends. Just as I haven't told Antoine what Iara explained to me about water paths, there are things he has kept quiet about too. It isn't so much that either of us is keeping secrets. It's just that there is only so much we both have room for, I guess. The twins are ours, an experience and a reality only he and I can truly understand. For the past few months, they have been all that has mattered, to either of us. The movements inside my growing belly and my strange, vivid dreams have been our own private joy, something we've wondered at and spent endless golden hours marveling over. It has been enough to know we're expecting not just one, but two miracles. I've been content to let the outside world move forward without me, and I suspect Antoine has felt the same.

That is about to change, though. Soon it won't be only our world that will concern us. Soon, the decisions we make will determine the course not only of our lives, but of those we are bringing into this world. The bodies inside my own shift and tumble as if the twins, too, are growing impatient. I think that whatever fears I have for Antoine and myself pale into insignificance when I weigh them against the future of our children, of the life we will give them.

"What is there to talk about?" Antoine steps away from me, his face grim. "We both agree you must be turned."

"Yes," I say gently. "We agreed it would happen right after the birth, as soon as the twins are free of my body." He shudders slightly, as if even my saying it aloud frightens him. "It's how it will happen that we need to discuss."

"You know how," he says harshly. "That isn't what you're asking me."

"No." I meet his eyes steadily. "It isn't." I take a deep breath. "I guess it's a question of *who*, rather than how."

Who will have to die so that I might live? Who is it that I will take into my body, to become part of my immortal soul? The slightest thought of taking a life by force horrifies me. "I haven't wanted to think about it either." I step closer to him, and this time Antoine doesn't step away. "The life that I take to become a vampire will become part of me," I say softly. "That person will be part of raising our children, Antoine. Part of me forever. We can't just pretend that doesn't matter."

One of his hands comes up and strokes the curls back from my face, twining them about the unruly pile gathered at the crown. "You're right," he says roughly, his hand cradling my head. "I know we need to talk about it, to make a plan. But I honestly don't know where to start, Harper."

My mouth twists. "It isn't like we can run an ad on Craigslist, is it?"

His own lips lift at the edges briefly. "Hardly."

The humor is gone as soon as it came, and we look at one another in the growing morning light. "We need to decide how we're going to do this, Antoine," I say quietly. "We've left it too late as it is. I can't go into this not knowing what is waiting for me on the other side. Can we agree that we have to talk about it at least?"

He nods slowly. "Agreed. But I'm not certain what talking about it will do."

I step further into his orbit, and he turns me so my back is against his chest, his hands holding my belly. I turn my head so my lips are against his jaw, just below his ear. "Talking about it will remind us that we are doing this together," I murmur against the heat of his skin. "That we aren't alone."

"Together." His arms tighten around me briefly. "Always," he murmurs.

"Always."

We stand as the day grows, and then we walk slowly up the slope together, our hands entwined.

~

TO DISTRACT MYSELF FROM MY OWN THOUGHTS, I HEAD BACK upstairs and prop myself up on my bed. I'm no more enthusiastic about unpacking the boxes from my old Baton Rouge life than I've ever been, but the impending arrival of the twins that has made me determined to at least open the more personal of them.

"Wow. I never thought I'd see the day." Callie perches on the end of my bed, grinning at me. I shoot her a slightly mutinous look. For someone with the ability to be entirely oblivious to the need for dishes to be washed, Callie possesses what to my mind is an unhealthy predilection for order. She has been dying to get her hands on the boxes in my room for months.

"I'm only doing a few," I say warningly. "Just the personal stuff. The ones—" I break off, realizing there is no nice way of saying what I was about to.

"The boxes you don't want other people opening after you're dead." Callie finishes the sentence for me. I open my mouth to reassure her that it's nothing of the kind, but when she raises her eyebrows, my lips twist ruefully.

"I guess." I slice open the tape. "We got left with a lot," I say apologetically. "Connor and I. First Mom's stuff, then Tessa's. I'd always planned to open Mom's boxes with Tessa, but then she got sick, and somehow, in the end, they all became one big mess that I couldn't face. I don't want to leave anyone with that mess if—" *and there it is again.* It seems there is no safe topic that doesn't somehow wind up back at my impending transformation.

"I can understand that." Callie smiles briefly, then turns matter of factly to the box. "So. Want privacy, or help?"

"Help. Definitely help." One of the things I love most about Callie is that she doesn't make a fuss.

It's oddly cathartic, pulling Mom's things out of the box. "They're Tessa's and my old christening robes." I lay them down carefully. "I remember Mom telling me they came over from Europe with some distant ancestor. Maybe we can use them for the twins. Oh, and this is one of those dumb teaspoons that have been handed down forever and given to newborn babies. I've never understood that custom."

The time passes in reminiscence and laughter, with a few poignant moments that are made easier by Callie's earthy practicality. Toward the end of the box, I find a velvet drawstring jewellery bag. "That's odd." I frown at it. "I thought Connor and

I had all the jewellery accounted for." The bag is better quality than those from a chain store, made from plush velvet and lined with satin. The only marking on it is a curlicued letter *R.* I'm certain I've never seen it before.

I turn it upside down, and two rings fall out.

"Wow." Callie picks one up, turning it over in her hand. "These are *so* cool."

"Do you think so?" I pick up the other one, examining it curiously. It's a wide silver band overlaid with ornamental silver detail, a series of joined *fleur de lys.* It has an old-fashioned feel, almost medieval, although that may be simply because the silver is so tarnished. I look at the matching bands critically. "They need a good clean."

"What's the writing on the inside?"

"I didn't notice any." I frown at the ring, trying to see what Callie is pointing at, but I can only make out a few worn lines.

"It's French." Callie is fascinated. "Hang on." Wiping the ring carefully with a corner of her shirt, she peers at it more closely. "*Qui vivra verra,*"she reads slowly. "It means: *he who lives shall see.*"

She looks up at me with a twisted smile. "That's weirdly appropriate."

"And so strange." I turn the rings over in my hand. "I honestly have no idea where they came from. I'm sure Mom never mentioned them."

"Well, they're in with all your baby stuff, so they're probably some kind of family heirloom." I catch the faintly wistful note in Callie's voice. "It must be nice," she says quietly. "To have so much family history. Things that have been handed down for generations." She colors, and her eyes slide away from mine. When she speaks again it's with a heavy dose of her old, tough accent. "Anythin' like that in our house, would've been pawned off long ago, but I'm guessin' weren't nothin' anyhow. All my Momma ever said 'bout family was that we was better off without 'em. Guessin' she was right, too."

Turning away, she starts chattering on about other things, but not before I see the unshed tears glistening in her eyes. Quietly I put the rings back in the bag, and tuck them away, out of sight.

~

You have just read a sample from Book #6 in the Nightgarden Saga. To keep reading, buy on Amazon.

AFTERWORD

Thankyou so much for reading Dusky Dahlia.

I hope you loved it!

If you did, please leave reviews on Goodreads, and Amazon. Reviews help indie authors more than you can imagine - I can't tell you how much I appreciate them.

You can download Antoine's story, a prequel to the Nightgarden Saga, at www.paulaconstant.com. It is free and exclusive to readers!

You can listen to the music that helped inspire the The Nightgarden Saga on Spotify.

Follow me on TikTok: @paulaconstant. Tag me in your review, and I will share and promote you!

You can also join the Nightgarden Readers Facebook group, and chat with others (and me) about the series.

If you would like to be the first to read and review advance copies of upcoming books, please visit www.paulaconstant.com and sign up.

To buy any of the books in the series, please go to Amazon.

If you would like a hardcopy for your insta or tiktok review, please email me at lucyholdenparanormal@gmail.com.

Thanks again.
Paula/Lucy

ABOUT THE AUTHOR

Lucy Holden is a pseudonym for Paula Constant, an Australian author who lives in the gorgeous north western pearling town of Broome. She adores gin martinis, dreaming on the beach beneath a full moon, and having pool book club with awesome friends. The name Lucy is taken from the girl who stepped through the wardrobe in the Narnia books, and Holden refers to Paula's beloved first car.

Paula is the author of historical fiction series the Visigoths of Spain, and travel memoirs Slow Journey South and Sahara.

www.paulaconstant.com

www.ingramcontent.com/pod-product-compliance
Lightning Source LLC
Chambersburg PA
CBHW010544170726
48285CB00008B/2735